"Hello Mr. Donahue." She ꞈ
Chris was standing with uncerꞈ
in a navy blue shirt and blue jeaꞈ
his pocket and he had a puzzled ι∪∪κ ∪n nis face.

"Hello, Miss Black," he answered gruffly. "How many bedrooms are in this house?"

"Three," Pinky said slowly and looking at him curiously.

"So where did Lance sleep?" Chris asked his hazel eyes fixed on her.

Pinky chuckled and answered sarcastically. "With me of course. The nights are very chilly now you know. A warm body is very welcomed."

Chris frowned. "Seriously?"

Pinky threw up her hands in the air. "What are you doing here?"

"I came to check up on you, " Chris said slowly, his head snapped up when a bare-chested guy stepped out on the veranda rubbing his eyes blearily.

"Where's my Pinkylicious, we were in the middle of something."

Pinky sighed. "Over here Lance."

Chris stiffened and glared at Lance hostilely. "I can't believe that you are carrying on like this in your parents' house."

"They endorsed it," Pinky said cheekily, "my mother even insisted on it."

Chris gasped. "You told me they were good Christian folks."

"They are," Pinky said grinning, "but every year at this time they allow me to do it."

IF IT AIN'T BROKE

BRENDA BARRETT

JAMAICA
TREASURES

IF IT AIN'T BROKE

A Jamaica Treasures Book/March 2013

Published by Jamaica Treasures
Kingston, Jamaica

This is a work of fiction. Names, characters, places, and incidents are either the product of the author's imagination or are used fictitiously. Any resemblance to an actual person or persons, living or dead, events, or locales is entirely coincidental.

Book Cover Design by Yorkali Walters

ISBN - 978-976-95566-0-7
Jamaica Treasures Ltd.
P.O. Box 482
Kingston 19
Jamaica W.I.
www.fiwibooks.com

Dear Reader

I really enjoyed writing the various characters in the Three Rivers Series. The series is set in Three Rivers, St. Ann, a little fictional town in Jamaica that is situated close to the famous Ocho Rios with its white sand beaches, verdant green mountains and lovely flowers.

The series starts out with Kelly, the pastor's wife, whose extra marital affair had far reaching consequences.

The second book in the series is about her sister, Erica, who is actively looking for a husband and had all but given up until she met the mysterious Caleb Wright who seemed to appear out of nowhere and had secrets he was afraid of sharing.

The third book is about Phoebe—whose main goal is to marry rich—she is forced to choose between Ezekiel who is rich but ugly, and Charles who is poor but handsome.

The final book in the series is about Chris who finds himself mysteriously drawn to his unsophisticated and opinionated housekeeper, while he battles the feelings he still harbors for Kelly.

Please, enjoy reading …

Yours Sincerely

Brenda Barrett

ALSO BY BRENDA BARRETT

DI TAXI RIDE AND OTHER STORIES
THE PULL OF FREEDOM
THE EMPTY HAMMOCK
NEW BEGINNINGS
FULL CIRCLE
LOVE TRIANGLE
THE PREACHER AND THE PROSTITUTE
PRIVATE SINS (THREE RIVERS)
LOVING MR. WRIGHT (THREE RIVERS)
UNHOLY MATRIMONY (THREE RIVERS)
IF IT AIN'T BROKE (THREE RIVERS)
HOMELY GIRL

ABOUT THE AUTHOR

Books have always been a big part of life for Jamaican born Brenda Barrett, she reports that she gets withdrawal symptoms if she does not consume at least two books per week. That is all she can manage these days, as her days are filled with writing, a natural progression from her love of reading. Currently, Brenda has several novels on the market, she writes predominantly in the historical fiction, Christian fiction, comedy and romance genres.

Apart from writing fictional books, Brenda writes for her blogs blackhair101.com; where she gives hair care tips and fiwibooks.com, where she shares about her writing life.

You can connect with Brenda online at:
Brenda-Barrett.com
Twitter.com/AuthorWriterBB
Facebook.com/AuthorBrendaBarrett

Chapter One

Chris eagerly sorted through the mail that was neatly arranged on the desk in his study. Today was Thursday, the day he got his weekly updates from his personal investigator in Cayman. His hands hovered over the manila envelope and then he put it aside for last.

He had other mail too. His eye caught a gold envelope with fancy lettering on the front. He picked it up contemplatively and sniffed the air; it smelled really sweet, like roses.

He opened it and saw an impressive invitation, "Chris Donahue and Guest: you are cordially invited to the nuptials of Ezekiel Abbas Hoppings and Phoebe Amita Bridge on Sunday, December 8 at the Lion's Gate Estate, Grand Cayman."

A tremor raced through Chris when he read the words Cayman, and then he spared a thought for Phoebe and Ezekiel—he was happy for them. He had seen his friend and neighbor recently. Ezekiel had looked so different and relaxed and extremely happy.

He ran his fingers through his hair and got up from the chair he had been sitting in.

It was as if a fat fist was cutting off his air when he thought of Cayman—he wondered if Ezekiel invited the Palmers. Wasn't he friends with Kelly?

It had been nearly three years since he last saw Kelly and he wondered if he would be seeing her face to face at the wedding.

And what if they brought his son? Was he supposed to act as if he didn't care when he saw him?

He had to decline this invitation, just as he had declined the invitation to Erica and Caleb's wedding. That one had been too close to home and he couldn't go through with it— who were they expecting him to carry anyway? He hadn't dated anyone since that disastrous few months with that clingy girl, Estella.

His mouth tightened in pain. His life so far had been work, work and more work. He had more money now than he ever had, but he was left with the cold dregs of unrequited love for a married woman who had his only child and was living happily with her husband in Cayman.

He lifted the brown envelope almost reluctantly, knowing he would be in a bad mood opening it. He wished his housekeeper wasn't around with her nosy concern. There was something about Pinky Black that made him angry too. She was defiant and nosy and didn't know the meaning of subservience, and her bright perkiness annoyed him. He had fired her twice before, and everyday since rehiring her he had thoughts about firing her again.

Chris looked at the envelope again. He was stalling, and for good reason. He always felt like a dirty voyeur who was punishing himself unnecessarily with the pictures he commissioned the detective to take of his young son and his mother. He had started having them trailed and photographed after finding himself in an extremely dark place on his son's first birthday.

Why should he just step back from his child's life? He needed to know how he was getting on—that the knowing was also punishment didn't matter to him.

He opened the envelope and there they were: a picture of Kelly and Mark walking on the beach. Kelly was in a sky blue maxi dress and his son was in swimming trunks with a bucket in hand. The boy had grown taller, taller than he looked in last week's photos. His hair was longer too, almost like a girl's, and curly. Mark's little cherubic cheeks had dimples. Chris felt his and again realized that his son was a miniature copy of himself.

Kelly was looking slimmer, and toned. He wondered if she was working out. Chris heaved a sigh, forcefully slammed down the thoughts of her from his mind and put the pictures back into the envelope.

He still held on to the thoughts of Kelly though, as his mind tortured him about the two of them. Usually he was eager to read the detective's report, but these days it was getting repetitive.

Last week Kelly took him to a kiddies' attraction, the week before that he had a cold. His heart had throbbed unnervingly until the detective reported that he was well again.

He loved his child and he wanted him. Not because of some selfish desire to break up Kelly's family but because the boy was his—his first born, and why was he the only one punished for that ill-fated affair?

Chris sighed, a big tremulous sigh that did nothing to loosen the tight fist that had taken permanent residence around his heart.

He was thinking that he would frame some of the pictures to track the development of his child. Then again maybe not, as that would mean everyday would be Thursday for him.

He heard a soft knocking on his study door, and he contemplated ignoring it, but knowing Pinky she would barge right in and bulldoze him with her overwhelming personality after trying the soft approach. He locked the manila envelope, along with its contents, into one of his desk's bottom draws.

"Come in," he said gruffly, bracing himself for his unconventional housekeeper.

Pinky popped her head around the door. "Hey boss man, I've got drama class tonight. Won't be around, ya dig?" She was chewing a gum as if she was going to murder it.

Chris sighed, "Pinky, how many times must I ask you not to refer to me as boss man."

"Four hundred and ninety," was the facetious reply. "I started counting it on my phone."

She came into the study fully and Chris inhaled sharply. "What on earth do you have on?"

Pinky looked down at herself. She was in very tight bike shorts and a red halter neck blouse.

"Do I look dangerous?" She purred and swayed her hips while walking up to Chris' desk. "My name is Fatima, the scandalous bar girl in the play."

Chris swallowed, watching her swaying hips head toward him. "Pinky, that outfit is too suggestive." He arranged his pants under the desk and struggled to remember what he was talking about.

"I know." Pinky winked at him with heavily made up eyelids. "My drama coach said, 'wear something skimpy and suggestive', so this is what I'm wearing. Wouldn't wear it on the street though, so please, no lectures. I have a dress that will be worn over it for class."

"And your hair?" Chris looked at her dazedly. Usually, Pinky had her hair cut in a spiky pixie cut which she dyed blonde. This time the tips were red like her blouse.

"Oh this," Pinky laughed, "is temporary...will wash out by tomorrow. I am going to run. Miss Maud said she cooked some gourmet dinner for you, can't remember the name of the dish. I don't want any. I'll pick up something after class."

"Wow, you are actually allowing me to have dinner alone?" Chris asked surprised. Pinky usually had dinner with Chris around the dining table and would normally take the opportunity to give him a ball-by-ball account of how her day went.

She had no respect for the employer/employee boundary. Rather than sit around the table—lonely and brooding—he had allowed her to do whatever she wanted. Usually she ate with him and talked to him about her day and had no qualms ferreting out information about his.

"There is this one guy," Pinky said, "the bad guy to my bad girl in drama class that I will persuade to take me to dinner— probably to a patty place. We are all broke students, he can't afford anything fancy."

A shaft of jealousy hit Chris out of nowhere and he actually inhaled with the suddenness of it. He was on the verge of forbidding Pinky to go out with the guy. So strong was the emotion gripping him that he actually forgot that it was Thursday. His mind had actually not been in Cayman.

He looked at Pinky wearily. "I need you to do something for me when you get back from class."

"What is it?" Pinky asked suspiciously.

"I need a...a...I need you to file some things for me…" Chris struggled with finding something to tell her to do.

"Well," Pinky put her hands on her hips unconsciously bracing out her chest, a look of fury in her eyes, "I never get to go anywhere or have any fun with you constantly on my case about stuff. 'Pinky do this for me, Pinky do that for me'."

"You are my housekeeper," Chris said incredulously, "have you forgotten that?"

Pinky frowned. "Yes, I had."

Then she laughed. "Sorry boss man. I will come home and do your urgent filing."

"Well," Chris leaned back in his chair, "I could collect you from drama class. It would save you the hassle of getting a cab to come back."

Pinky grinned at him cheekily. "Or, I could drive one of the cars in your garage."

Chris frowned, "not after you dented my Mercedes' fender."

"It was not my fault," Pinky gasped. "The other guy was not looking where he was going."

"I am going to have to find a cheaper car for you to drive around. Until then, I'll collect you from class."

Pinky huffed. "I can't believe that you don't trust me to drive your precious Merc." She stormed out of the study, her pert rear end swaying seductively.

"What time does class end?" Chris called after her retreating back.

"Six o' clock," Pinky said, "and don't park at the front gate like you did last time. Don't want anybody to think that I have a rich boyfriend. You had tongues wagging the last time you parked at the front and leaned on the car waiting for me. The girls started envying me and the boys stopped flirting with me."

Chris nodded contemplatively and decided to park at the front of her school. He felt inordinately pleased that the boys had stopped flirting with her.

*****

Pinky looked through her classroom window, and there he was. He was there at six o' clock on the dot, and couldn't have been more conspicuous if he tried—his curly hair, that sexy dimple when he smiled, those gorgeous eyes. She drunk him in and sighed.

She had it extremely bad for her boss. She had tried every trick in the book to get him to notice that she was a woman, but they all fell woefully flat. At least she had goaded him into picking her up, she thought triumphantly. She also hadn't missed that spark of jealousy that he had in his eye when she spoke about Brandon.

Poor Brandon. As if she would have gone out with him, especially since his girlfriend, Tracy, was her friend and study partner. But she had been grasping at straws to get Chris Donahue to notice that she exists.

How could one man be so thick?

She growled in frustration.

"Aren't you coming out?" Tracy asked her, then she glanced through the window. "Your delicious drop-dead handsome boss is outside waiting to pick you up."

Pinky sighed, "my delicious drop-dead-handsome boss is married to a memory. Alas, I'm out in the cold where his affections are concerned."

Tracy looked her over. "I don't buy it. You have a pretty face, a nice shape. You are young and healthy—Is he gay?"

"Nope." Pinky said gathering up her bag. "He's straight, it's just that his mind is occupied by another woman. See you Monday for Computational Chemistry class. Can't wait until the end of semester to get this course over and done with.

One semester to go and then we are out of here for good. Chemistry degree.

Yay!"

Tracy high-fived her, and they trouped out together.

*****

She got into the car with Chris, who had opened the door for her with a smirk on his face. "So the guy in the glasses, who walks kind of lean, is the bad guy you were going out with?"

Pinky laughed. "Why is this of interest to you boss?"

"Because I need to know what my housekeeper is up to in her spare time," Chris said seriously.

"Have you ever asked Miss Maud what she's up to in her spare time?" Pinky asked cheekily.

Miss Maud was the overweight cook that Chris inherited from his parents. She lived in a cottage on the property but spent most of her time in the kitchen.

"I know what she's up to." Chris looked over at Pinky and laughed. "She's eating enough for the three of us combined."

Pinky laughed. "She baked a cake yesterday. I got a sliver of a piece."

"I didn't get any," Chris said. "So, you do have fun. Your pretense that I'm a slave driver is ridiculous."

"I am twenty-one," Pinky said, "I live in a big house with you and old Maud and Griffin the cat. I have had no life since I started working for you."

"And I've had no fur-free slippers since you brought that stray-puss into my house," Chris said ignoring her outburst. "Anyway, how would you like to go to a wedding in Cayman with me as my date?"

"Oh really?" Pinky's eyes lit up. "You are asking me as

your date. Me— Pinky Black as your date. Oh wow!"

"Oh, Pinky," Chris said, "sorry to burst your bubble but the invitation said Chris Donahue plus one and since I'm not seeing anybody and you said you were not having any fun, I thought this would be a good opportunity for you to have some fun, in another country."

"I don't care how you want to pretty it up, you are asking me on a date. I am going to dance a little when I get out of the car. Whose wedding is it by the way?"

"Ezekiel Hoppings and Phoebe Bridge. I think you know Phoebe, she dated your brother."

"Of course I know Phoebe," Pinky said excitedly, "I like her. I knew she wasn't right for my brother but I'm so happy for her. How cool is that? I'll get to go to her wedding in Cayman. Woohoo! I have got to tell my friends about this."

"Er..." Chris looked at her smiling face; she was almost bouncing off the car seat in glee. "You have my permission to buy yourself a new outfit for the wedding—charge it to the household expenses account."

"Are you kidding me?" Pinky squealed. "I am going to the most expensive store in town."

Chris grinned. "Knock yourself out."

"Thanks boss man," Pinky said happily. "Does this mean that we are a couple now?"

"Not on your life," Chris said driving slowly up his driveway.

It was only when he was once again sitting in his study, after finding some documents for Pinky to file, that he realized that he had completely forgotten about his Thursday doldrums. He hadn't thought about Kelly or Mark, not even once. Pinky Black was having a very unusual effect on him.

Chapter Two

Chris stood out on his room's balcony at a private guesthouse on Cayman's East End. He had rented the whole property for a week but he only intended to stay for the wedding and then head back home—just being in close proximity to his son and Kelly made him uncomfortable.

He inhaled deeply and glanced at his watch. It was just eight o' clock in the evening. A slight breeze was coming from the sea; there was an invasive chill in the air. He felt almost cold.

He could hear Pinky giggling to some sitcom she was watching in the lounge area and he thought about joining her. He was reluctant to be alone with his thoughts just now.

They had arrived earlier that evening and he had picked up his rental car at the airport. While driving to the East End, he had asked himself why he had decided to come to Cayman and torture himself. Theo and Kelly lived right here on the

East End. Almost ten minutes from where he was staying now.

He knew their address by heart. If he could just walk up the beach from where he was standing now, he would be within spitting distance of their home. The beach where the P.I. had taken their picture two months ago was now a stones throw from where he was standing. Probably Theo and Kelly had even passed where he was now staying to go walking. It was a nice stretch of beach.

He had to admit that this was a perfect place to bring up a child. The life on the East End was peaceful and slow paced. He could imagine them splashing around in the sea and having family picnics. His thoughts were making him melancholy. He heard the television turned down and the sound of Pinky's slippers heading toward his door.

He had not been the best of company for the day. The closer they had come to Cayman the grumpier he had gotten; he had merely grunted when Pinky made observations in her over exuberant way.

He allowed himself a small smile, but that hadn't stopped her. She had commented like a one-man radio all the way to the guesthouse and then she had grabbed her overnight bag and taken the biggest room, which also had a view of the sea.

"Oh Sir, Bossman," she called through the door, "are you going to be in a bad mood for much longer, or do you want to watch Star Trek with me? Better yet, let's go somewhere touristy and act like we are foreigners—which we are." She giggled.

Chris pushed himself away from the balcony and headed toward his room door. Maybe it was not such a bad idea after all—to have some company—especially leading up to this wedding. Chris drew the door open and Pinky almost fell in. Her ear was pressed to the door.

She had changed into a hot pink summery looking dress. Her big brown eyes were gazing at him inquisitively and he felt a brief urge to grab her and kiss her, throw her on the bed and use her to forget.

He slammed the thought down and scowled at her fiercely. "I am not in the mood to go anywhere, Petrina Black."

Pinky smiled slowly. "You are using my right name. How utterly formal and distinguished I sound when you say it like that—Petrina Black."

She leaned on the doorjamb. "I can't believe that you dragged me from Jamaica to come to Cayman just so that I can watch TV alone.

Chris sighed, "you're right, but unfortunately for you, there is really no night life here on the East End. Unless you want to go to a restaurant?"

"Not hungry," Pinky shrugged. "Maud packed such a wad for us to carry over here, that one would think we are spending the whole year. Let's go watch TV then. I carried my chemistry book to study for finals but my mind is not on it. I keep wishing it was morning so that I can see the spectacular views outside."

Chris shrugged. "Okay, after you. Though I think I have watched most of the Star Trek episodes already."

Pinky lead the way to the sitting room and sat in one of the overstuffed chairs. "I can't believe you don't have property here. This is a really nice place to live."

"I do have property here." Chris sat beside her, their thighs almost touching. He looked at her legs; they were smoothly shaven and looked golden.

"Pinky."

"Hmm." Pinky said glancing at him.

"You are not going to wear skimpy clothes to the wedding tomorrow are you?"

Pinky snorted. "No. I bought a stunning dress. I have never spent so much money for one item of clothing before. But I figured since you grudgingly asked me to come, and wanted to make a good impression on your friends, to prove to them that you are not a sad lonely man that needs to carry his housekeeper as a date," she shrugged. "I bought an elegant knockout just to show them boss man, don't worry."

Chris sighed. "Thank God for that, and I'm not a sad lonely man."

"Yes, you are," Pinky said, "you have been grouchy since you told me about the wedding. I was wondering why but then I came up with one reason. It has something to do with that certain female, whose name I am not allowed to call or I'll be fired. Her name begins with K and ends with elly."

Chris looked at her sideways and then heaved a sigh. "You are too perceptive for your own good."

"You are too burdened for your own good." Pinky looked at the television screen; the images melding together as she formulated her thoughts. "But I hope you realize that you can tell me what has you so tied up inside. I am a good listener and willing to help, and I won't even charge you overtime."

Chris looked at her long and hard; her blond hair was in little curls all over her head. Near up he could see the evenness of her skin tone and the curve of her lips.

"I will bear that in mind, Petrina Black."

Pinky smiled showing him her straight white teeth.

*****

The wedding was at Lion's Gate on Ezekiel's sprawling 45,000 sq. ft property; about fifteen minutes drive from where they were staying. It was a ten o' clock wedding which was supposed to be held in the courtyard. Chris had been to

Lion's Gate before; he remembered it as a magnificent house.

"I can't believe that Phoebe is getting married today," Pinky said beside him incredulously. "I spoke to my brother last night and he is going to be here too. Phoebe actually arranged for his entire band to be flown in today. Can you imagine?"

Chris grunted.

"And her friends Erica and Tanya are going to be brides maids, even though Erica had her baby six weeks ago."

Chris glanced over at her; she was applying lip-gloss to her already shiny lips. He had to admit that she looked as elegant as she said she would. She had on a hunter green dress with a modest neckline and intricate beadwork around the neck area. She was also wearing matching shoes with a brown bag to match.

Even her usually wild looking hair was somewhat tamed into a curly blond style—it suited her. In fact, she looked extremely pretty. He would have told her so after he had found himself gaping at her when she came downstairs earlier that morning. But in usual Pinky style she had waltzed downstairs, gushed how handsome he was and told him that she had chosen to wear green so that when she was near his hazel eyes would pick up the color.

"We are going to be quite the couple boss man." She had announced.

He smiled slightly. Pinky was like a force of nature. When he saw her this morning the dark level of despair that he had felt in anticipation of seeing Theo and Kelly had subsided into a mist.

He was calmly heading toward Lions Gate and wondering where all the anxiety that had him tossing and turning last night had gone.

"Is your friend Caleb going to be there?" Pinky asked him,

capping her lip-gloss and smiling in his direction.

"Definitely," Chris said nodding, "he is on babysitting duty. As you said Erica is a part of the wedding party. She won't have much time to attend to the baby."

"Oh," Pinky said glancing through the window, "is she—who cannot be named—attending the wedding?"

Chris tensed. "She is friends with Ezekiel. She might be there."

"Small world," Pinky said tensely. "Do you still have feelings for her?"

Chris turned into the driveway leading to the beach side mansion and absentmindedly handed the security the invitation.

The question rang in his mind and gave him a weak helpless feeling of despair. He had told himself several times that he was over Kelly, but was he really?

He had not taken out his feelings and examined them close up for a long time. He had put his emotions on icy lockdown for so long now that he kind of resented Pinky asking him about them.

She was looking at him fearfully as if she expected him to blow at any minute.

"I don't know." He smiled at her when he said it, hoping to impart to her that he was fine. He wasn't sure the smile reached his eyes.

Pinky exhaled, "okay." Then she looked around her surroundings and gasped. "This is serious luxury."

Chris chuckled. "Promise me you won't say anything outrageous to the people here."

Pinky giggled. "I won't say a thing out of the way boss. I promise to keep my speech free of slang. If I see celebrities I won't hunt them down for an autograph, but I may beg them for a picture."

Chris sighed. "That's all I ask."

*****

The courtyard was beautifully decorated in white and gold. There were hundreds of white roses everywhere. There were two columns of chairs all facing a fancily decorated wedding arch that were facing the sea. The air was heady with the scent of the roses. Quite a few persons were already there and seated. It was not as big a wedding as Pinky had thought it was going to be. She counted about two hundred chairs.

Pinky sat beside a girl named Vanessa who said she was a former co-worker of Phoebe's. She was especially glad that Vanessa, who was sitting to the right of her, was so friendly because Chris was staring tensely into space.

She knew that he was holding himself tautly because she glanced at him every three minutes to see if he was all right—his jaw was constantly clenched. She could not imagine the kind of anxiety and stress he was going through at the moment.

He looked so handsome though, with his cleanly shaven jaw and those clear hazel eyes. He was in a black tux and she thought how magnificent he looked.

She felt really privileged that she was sitting beside him as his 'date'. She wished it were real though, that they were really dating and that he was intensely in love with her and not Kelly.

She was anxious to see Kelly, that paragon of virtue that Chris held in such high esteem. In a way she was just as anxious to see her as Chris was. Maybe, if she could pinpoint the one thing that made Kelly so attractive to Chris she could emulate it.

Pinky didn't even know if that theory was workable.

Though Chris' emotions were thoroughly engaged, she knew that human emotions were a mass of contradictions. Maybe what was attractive to him in Kelly would be totally abhorrent with her.

What would make Chris be so fixated on one woman for most of his life? She pondered the question for all of five minutes and then she shrugged inwardly—that's why chemistry was her area of study and not psychology.

"This is really spectacular," Vanessa was saying to Pinky.

Pinky nodded. "It is. I never knew that places like this exist outside of fairy tales."

Vanessa laughed. "Me either. And to imagine, Phoebe gave up all of this when she wasn't sure that she loved Ezekiel. That is admirable."

Pinky smiled. "It was."

She saw a flash of red and black and realized that her brother and his band had arrived.

"Hey Charles," she said loudly and waved wildly.

Charles spun around, and waved at her. He came over a grin on his face.

"Hey, you guys are early. "

"The wedding is scheduled to start at ten," Chris said, glancing at his watch, "it's five to ten."

Charles shrugged. "Phoebe told me that her mother insisted on her wearing some elaborate wedding gown that will take about five hours to get into."

"Is that so?" Chris asked appalled. "If I had known this little tidbit of information, I would have come twelve o' clock instead."

Charles shrugged, "Phoebe said she was going to defy her and wear something else. We'll see who wins that war. Besides, Tanya and Erica are her bridesmaids and they are not really known for their patience. I am going to set up for the reception. Apparently there'll be some fancy violinist doing the ceremony. See ya later Sis and I must say you look really good."

"Thank you," Pinky grinned. "You dear boy."

Charles rolled his eyes. "Why are you talking so fancy?"

"My boss insisted on it." She glanced at Chris.

"Oh," Charles grinned, looking at Chris' tight expression, "talk to you later."

They didn't have long to wait for the wedding to start. The groom came out standing beside the minister and his best man. They were dressed in white and were relaxed and laughing.

"Oh my God," Chris said, a strained look to his mouth.

"What?" Pinky asked anxiously.

"The minister," Chris said strangled, "why didn't I think of that? Why didn't I think that he would be their minister? There she is." He whispered.

Pinky craned her neck to see who he was going on about. The minister was a handsome guy dressed in a black tux similar to Chris'. He had a sprig of white in his lapel.

"Where is she?" Pinky asked anxiously.

Then she saw her, without Chris having to describe her. She was wearing a multicolored silky dress in a halter-top style. She had long natural curly hair. Deep brown complexion and she was looking over the crowd too.

She wanted to see if Chris was around but she was playing it casual Pinky surmised. She was doing it furtively just like she would have.

Pinky knew the exact moment that Kelly's eyes found Chris. She looked directly behind and then at Chris, her eyes widened a bit and even at the distance Pinky could see her tense up.

Pinky imagined that she could feel the electricity in the air.

Chris was tenser than ever and his eyes were drinking her in like a lost puppy. She felt like grabbing his shoulders and shaking him to get him out of his Kelly-induced trance.

Kelly was the first one to break eye contact and Chris was still staring in her direction like a statue.

"Stop it," Pinky said exasperated, "she is married remember?"

Chris slowly closed his eyes and exhaled, his first eye contact with Kelly was not as traumatic as he thought it would have been. All of that angst and build up over her and it wasn't as bad as he thought it was going to be. The sharp pain he had been tensing up for had only been a dull thud.

He opened his eyes and smiled at a concerned looking Pinky. "Relax. I am okay."

Pinky subsided in her chair. "Glad to hear."

A lone violinist walked slowly to the front playing Canon in D. Behind him walked the bridesmaids in gold gowns and then the bride in a simple white sari wedding dress with gold threads running through the material. It seemed as if the morning light glinted off her in a golden glow.

The crowd actually gasped when she appeared. She carried a lone rose and a peaceful smile.

The groom had tears in his eyes when he saw her and he met her halfway down the aisle.

Pinky rummaged in her bag for her handkerchief. She did not want her mascara to run but she could see the raw love on Ezekiel's face when he looked at Phoebe, and that created a yearning within her that she didn't even know she had.

The whole ceremony was a tearful one. The bride and groom took turns tearing up. The vows were so solemn and inspiring. Pinky found herself sniffing several times and had to borrow a wet wipe from Vanessa to dab at her eyes. Chris looked at both of them in disgust.

"I am never going to a wedding with you again," he whispered to Pinky when it was over. "What are you sniffing about?"

Pinky swatted him with her kerchief. "It was just so beautiful when they looked into each others eyes and they wrote the vows to each other themselves. It was poetic and romantic," she sniffed.

Chris looked up in the air. "Women."

Pinky pouted. "I am not the only romantic here, Mr. Donahue, you have loved the same woman for years. Who is the hopeless romantic here?"

Chris looked at her sharply. "Don't bring that up now. We still have the reception to go through."

"Okay, alright," Pinky said shakily. "Let's go congratulate the bride and the groom."

Chapter Three

Chris found himself in the mini orchard before the reception began. Pinky had dragged him in there because she had spotted Tanya and Erica. He had reluctantly gone along, though he had seen several business acquaintances he could have tarried with and made polite chatter.

Tanya and Erica were standing beside Caleb who was holding his daughter. Beside him stood Kelly and Theo with their children and his son.

It was his worst nightmare come through.

He had actually stopped when he saw them standing around in their little group.

His son was in Theo's arms with his head on a shoulder; a small trusting hand around his neck.

When he stopped, everybody looked around and the conversation ceased. It was as if all the background noises had faded too and there was only silence. He silently cursed Pinky in his mind for allowing him to walk into this trap.

"Hey Chris," Caleb said loudly coming toward him. Coming to his rescue. Chris' eyes had stopped on the toddler's hand around Theo's neck and they couldn't move away. It was as if they were fixated.

He hadn't seen Mark with Kelly in the service. He had assumed he wasn't there. How wrong he was. His heart and head were scrambling all over the place. He didn't know what to think, or where to look, or how to feel.

His flesh and blood was right near him, just ten paces away and he couldn't touch him or acknowledge him in anyway. The pain that he had expected to feel on seeing Kelly slammed into him when he saw his son.

"Just walk away man," Caleb was saying to him seriously.

Pinky who had eagerly run over to Tanya and Erica had sensed the tension and was wondering why the dramatic pause when she followed Chris' eyes and saw the little boy. She could read a wealth of pain in Chris' eyes. When the little boy raised his head and she saw his eyes—so identical to Chris'—she understood so much more than she had before.

For Chris, Kelly was not just an unrequited love. She had been his lover and the mother of his child.

Tanya whistled under her breath, "uh oh."

Pinky felt like echoing that but she valiantly kept her mouth shut.

Erica grabbed Tanya's hand. "Let's get out of here, we have pictures to take after the bride and groom are finished with their personal photo session."

"But that's not yet," Tanya protested, her eyes darting around the frozen milieu, "can't we stay?"

Erica pinched her and pulled her away. "Come Matthew and Thea."

The children had stopped their chatter when the adults had all stood around tense but they followed their aunt obediently.

Thea looked behind at her parents curiously but Erica was right behind her, prompting them to leave.

Pinky was left standing in the mini orchard, with its overhead glass ceiling and grape vines, feeling as if she was caught in the middle of something for which she had no preparation. Caleb had not gotten through to Chris, who was still standing his ground and staring at the toddler.

"Come on man," Caleb was urging Chris.

Chris looked at him and cleared his throat. "This had to happen sooner or later."

Caleb shrugged. "Okay then. I am going to be outside in the reception hall."

Chris sauntered closer to Kelly and Theo. He was emanating a confidence that he was far from feeling. Theo had a frown in his eyes, a keep off look that was annoying Chris slightly. They were all adults here, what did they expect him to do? Run off and avoid them both like he was some sort of prima donna? There was one lesson that his father had taught him when growing up that had stuck, it was that he had to stand and face difficult situations like a man.

"You know," Chris drawled casually, "I always thought that in this whole situation I was the one being punished the harshest."

Theo cleared his throat. "Chris you promised to stay away from us."

Kelly shrank closer to her husband as if being too close to Chris was contaminating her somehow.

Chris pushed his hand in his pocket and affected a casual pose. "Pinky, you see why I was so solemn when I came to Cayman? This is my son, Mark, and these are the people who are raising him without my input. It seems a bit unfair doesn't it?"

Kelly and Theo spun around and looked at Pinky. They

had not realized that she was there; so tense they were when Chris had walked into the room.

Pinky cleared her throat. "Maybe I shouldn't be in here now. I... er... excuse me."

She left the three of them reluctantly.

"Daddy, can I go find Mafew and Thea?" Mark spun around and looked at the strange man who was gazing at him.

Theo set him on his feet and straightened up watching as Mark toddled over to Chris, his upturned face looked so innocent and trusting.

Chris hunkered down to his level. "Hello, little one."

Mark backed off and went back to Theo, hugging his feet.

Chris stood up—a pain, so sharp, hitting him somewhere in the region of his heart. Mark didn't know him, Chris reminded himself, even though he felt as if he knew the boy from all the PI pictures. He was just a stranger to his son.

A strange man and he would ever be a strange man if the hostility that he could feel coming from Kelly were any indication. Curiously, Theo was not as hostile. He was contemplating him with an unidentifiable look in his gaze.

Kelly sighed, breaking the silence. "Chris, this is supposed to be a happy day. Let's not spoil it with our past issues."

Chris raised his eyebrows. "I'm not doing anything," he sneered, "and our past issues, are very much present."

He looked down at Mark his eyes softening perceptibly.

"We had a conversation almost three years ago Chris," Theo said authoritatively, "you promised to stay away from my family."

Chris nodded. "I know, and I have. But I have been thinking about it and this whole staying away from you business is making me unhappy. I have realized that it's not as easy to dismiss your own flesh and blood from your mind as casually as one would hope. I think about him every single day."

"But Chris," Kelly said a sob in her voice, "it has been three years. Why haven't you moved on?"

"Because I can't." Chris looked at Mark again and shrugged. "Any man worth his mettle cannot just move on from his own child."

He spun around and left the three of them in the mini orchard.

*****

He hardly remembered anything much about the reception. There were many toasts and much laughter but Chris couldn't bring himself to crack a smile.

Pinky had even volunteered to drive them home and he had dropped the keys in her palm without protest. There was a sadness weighing upon him that was like a physical presence.

Pinky must have felt its presence too because she hardly said a word when they reached the guesthouse. Her eyes were wet as if she had been crying and she was giving him one of her cautious looks.

"You aren't planning to do anything...you know...foolish?" she asked him fearfully.

"Like what," Chris shrugged, "break into their house in the dead of night and steal my son?"

"Well, I was thinking throwing yourself off the balcony in broken despair."

Chris rolled his eyes. "You like high drama don't you?"

He flung himself down in the lounge settee and said mockingly in a television announcer's voice. "The tragic Chris, heart broken and mourning over the mess he has made of his life. Gives it up in a blaze of passionate heart break, throwing himself over the balcony of his rented Guest

House, his last words were, 'I am undone'."

Pinky giggled nervously. "You just looked so sad. Like all the stuffing is gone out of you."

"It has," Chris said closing his eyes and massaging his temples. "I shouldn't have come to this wedding. I should have stayed away. I knew I'd see them, but I wanted them to see me. I wanted the two of them to remember that while they are playing happy family with my child, I am still hurting… still real…still the father. Not some phantom break in their marriage that they can paper over and hope for the best. Did you hear how Mark called Theo his Daddy?"

Pinky nodded and then cleared her throat after realizing that he wasn't looking at her. "Yes...er...Chris. How did this whole thing between you and Kelly happen? She's a pastor's wife. I was so shocked when I saw that little boy."

"I met her before Theo did." Chris laughed bitterly. "I loved her first. She was mine until she met Theo. Then one day, she called me over the phone—it was a Wednesday afternoon— she said in that husky voice of hers, 'Chris, I am marrying Theo'. I almost collapsed, but I survived. I reasoned that time had a way of healing things and that I could move on."

He cracked an eye open, "but I never did. In all the years while she was married, I never healed. I had an affair with her. Yes, I knew it was wrong, but I reasoned that it was my only chance with her. I ignored my conscience; I ignored everything really. Then she got pregnant. At first I thought she was pregnant for her husband and that tore me up inside. You know...sour grapes...but one look at the baby and I knew that he was mine."

He sighed and closed his eyes again, "I thought she'd leave him and we'd be happy together, but apparently he loves her enough to forgive her trespasses. Can you imagine?"

Pinky sighed. "That's quite unusual. Men are the ones who

are on the receiving end of forgiveness more often than not."

Chris loosened his bow tie.

"I once wrote a poem to Kelly when we were dating and I was under the illusion that we would be together forever. It said, 'if hearts had locks you'd be my key. If I were your slave I'd never be free. I'd dot every I, I'd cross every T. If that was the only way you could be mine, Kelly'."

"Awww," Pinky said enviously, "it sounds corny but sweet. I wish someone would write me a poem like that. You know what I think about all of this?"

Chris opened his eyes fully and looked at her. "No, what?"

"I think she is the one that got away. People usually are fixated on what they have lost. Build dreams around it; make it more than it is. Maybe if the two of you had married, you would have been miserable together."

Chris shook his head and got up. "We leave tomorrow at nine. Be ready."

"That's it?" Pinky asked to his retreating back.

"I've heard it all before," Chris mumbled, "I don't want to hear it again."

"You just love being unhappy and miserable," Pinky shouted after him.

He slammed his door in response.

Chapter Four

When Pinky got back from Cayman, two days later she found herself almost as depressed as Chris and he was zombie-like. She felt a heaviness in the air that did not bode well for her final exams in Computational Chemistry. For her, the subject was the most challenging she had to do the entire semester. She had barely passed the pre-requisite course and now she was struggling to remember the formulas and calculations that she learned in Physical Chemistry.

She found herself staring at her computer and wondering what molecules and solids were. Basic computations were tying her up in knots even though she was trying as hard as she could to concentrate, but it was useless.

She had taken her laptop with her into the garden where she thought she could get away from her thoughts about Chris and his mood and his love for Kelly. But in the cool of the day, with only the rustling leaves for company, peace eluded her.

She thought that she could get back to her studies but even here she felt troubled. She had learned far more about Chris and his obsession with Kelly than she wanted to but she still felt herself reeling over the whole thing.

It was one thing to come around to the fact that the man that you loved or had a thing for loved another woman obsessively. It was quite another thing to suddenly realize that he had an affair with her and had a baby.

Why is it that she hadn't even heard the whisper of this from anyone else, even that time when she had been ranting and raving about Chris? Phoebe had not once let it slip that he was the father to Kelly's youngest child, but she must have known about it. She had been staying at Kelly's house.

It must be the best-kept secret in Three Rivers because she had not once heard about it. She sighed heavily and got up from the wrought iron table, which was conveniently located under a sprawling cashew tree.

Pinky paced between the back wall—which had a view of the bay—and the table where her computer was waiting with her chemistry work, its metallic screen gazing at her accusingly.

She always thought that she had a chance with Chris, but now she realized that she had been wasting her time trying to be his friend and waiting patiently for him to notice that he was a man and that she was an attractive woman and that Kelly was not around. The whole situation was deeper than she had bargained for.

Even this job as housekeeper was really to get closer to Chris. She remembered the first time she saw him, she had been job-hunting for a part-time position that could supplement her scholarship. She had heard, from a friend at Great Pond church that Meghan who worked at Villa Rose wanted someone to fill in for her for about six weeks. She had eagerly gone to the Villa and waited for an impromptu interview with Chris Donahue that Meghan had arranged.

Earlier when she had sat apprehensively in the reception area, a handsome guy with pale green eyes had strutted pass her and she had stared at him her mouth hanging open. He had glanced at her contemplatively and then briskly went about his business, strutting with the confident air of someone important or in charge. That one look had had her feeling warm and tingly all over. When she actually got the chance to go into the conference room for the interview, she realized that he was her interviewer.

He had been brisk and business-like and somewhat cold toward her. She had thought that she would not have gotten the job. He had asked her questions and then sat back in his chair just listening to her tie up herself with some of the hardest ones.

He hadn't even cracked a smile when she had gotten up to leave. He had briskly shaken her hand and then escorted her outside.

When he called her the next day and asked her to come in, she had been extremely surprised and equally delighted to have the chance to work with him. Not that working with him had done her any good. He had kept his distance from her. When he worked from his office at Villa Rose he usually gave her brusque hellos and even terser goodbyes.

When Meghan came back from sick leave, he had asked her if she wanted to work as his housekeeper.

"My mother says I need one," Chris had shrugged. "A cleaning firm comes in every Friday, I have a cook, Maud. She was a gourmet chef in another century. I guess you can spread the bed, make sure my casual clothes are clean, pick-up my dry cleaning and any other odd jobs around the place.

I am hardly there, it's not much work and you can finish your final year in university without much fuss."

Pinky had been shocked. He had up to that point barely paid her any attention, except for a faint sneer in his eyes when he spoke to her. She found it quite astounding that he remembered that she was in her final year at university. She had tried to look nonchalant when he offered her the position but she had been extremely happy.

She'd be close to him every day. There was no way he could be exposed to her and not like her back. She would make it her mission, and what a task she had set for herself. She had bulldozed her way into his life. She purposely ignored his insults and acted as outrageously as she could to get his attention.

She had always been aware that there was a Kelly who held his heart in her hands. She had gotten that name from the gardener who had worked with Kelly when she designed the hotel.

He had told her bits and pieces of information about Kelly and how she was the woman who had so tied up Chris' emotions that he was very unavailable to all newcomers.

It was a few weeks after working with Chris that she had heard that Kelly was unavailable because she was married. And it was just three days ago that she found out that Kelly had been much more than unrequited love. She was the mother of his child.

Pinky plucked at her tube top in despair. What was she to do in a situation like this? She had been working for Chris for about a year now. Seven months ago she had told him to get over Kelly and quietly hoped that he would choose her instead. She had left the thought unspoken, but she was sure that Chris got the message.

He had chosen to fire her instead. He had been furious at

what he described as 'her temerity to be forthright about his personal life.'

Three days later, after he had calmed down, he had asked her to come back with a terse apology. She still wanted to be close to him so she had accepted. She had vowed never to speak of Kelly again and for a while she had imagined, fondly, that Chris was beginning to like her back.

He certainly acted jealous when she told him about the guys she knew at school but now she realized that she had been building castles in the sky.

Chris was nowhere near ready to get over his obsession with Kelly; this weekend was a cruel reminder of that. As a matter of fact his utter despair since he got back was telling. It had not been easy to hear that Chris had written poems to Kelly, that they had an affair, or that she had his son.

She got up to pace again—eaten up with jealousy. The green-eyed monster was riding her back; clouding her brain waves; making it impossible for her to concentrate.

Just one semester to go and then she would get that chemistry degree—an admirable feat for a girl who was born in deep rural Hanover with parents who were humble folks with barely a formal education.

Her mother sold the farm produce from the family farm and her father spent his time in the fields. She would be the only one in her family to have a college degree; her brother, Charles, had recently shown some interest in school so she might have company in a few years.

She didn't want to spoil this opportunity that she had, she had come too far to flunk a course and losing her scholarship all because Chris Donahue was tying her up in knots.

"Why are you pacing and carrying on like that?" Maud asked. She was carrying a tray with iced tea and what looked like pastries.

"Just thinking," Pinky said dejected.

Maud set the tray down on the table, glanced in her opened textbook and shook her head. "That looks like gibberish."

Pinky gave her a half-smile.

"Since you two got back from Cayman, the house has been like a funeral parlor," Maud said sitting down in a chair and helping herself to a pastry. "I had to catch myself this morning from wailing Rock of Ages Cleft For Me. It is Three Rivers Church's favorite funeral song."

"Do you know anything about Kelly?" Pinky asked her abruptly.

Maud almost choked on her pastry. "Uh huh."

Pinky smirked. "Well, we saw her."

"And the child too?" Maud asked wiping her eyes.

"Yup." Pinky picked up one of the pastries and started chewing dejectedly.

Maud shook her head sadly. "His mother was livid when she found out that Chris was not going to fight to keep the child."

Pinky's eyes lit up. "She was?"

"Yeah." Maud reached for another pastry, her pudgy fingers curving around it, "But I thought that since you were here, Chris was moving on. I haven't seen him laugh so much or have more life."

Pinky shrugged. "He doesn't like me."

Maud looked at her contemplatively. "It's plain to whoever who wants to see that that isn't true."

Pinky sighed bitterly. "I highly doubt that. To him I am just a young puppy; he doesn't treat me much different than he does the cat. That's it. I am just like a pet."

"Anyways," Maud said getting up, "Miss Camille and her husband are coming next week. She usually stays for two months; her husband stays for three weeks. This place will be quite busy for the next few weeks, so you are going to have your work cut out for you. I hope you can juggle that and your exams."

Pinky shrugged. "I will be done with all my exams by December 22. My last semester is mostly lab work."

"Okay." Maud shrugged.

"What is Camille like?" Pinky asked interestedly. She knew that Chris had three sisters who lived in Canada and that Camille was the closest to him.

"She's nice," Maud said, "very protective of her brother. They all are. Chris is the baby among bossy women but usually he holds his own. It is quite fun to see when the whole Donahue brood get together. I baby-sat all of them at some point or the other," Maud said lovingly. "Anyway, get back to your work, let me not keep you."

She waddled away her square behind retreating into the house. Pinky watched her silently and glanced at her laptop and textbook and closed both of them angrily.

She would never be a part of the Donahue clan if Chris didn't get his head out of Kelly-heaven; somehow the thought made her extremely sad, even more morose than she was before.

*****

Chris left the office early. It was Thursday and he expected his usual package from Cayman. He was already in a dark mood. He hadn't slept much since the confrontation with Theo and Kelly in Cayman. He had just been going through the motions. He could remember Kelly's incredulous question—"why haven't you moved on?"

The nerve of her.

When she had chosen Theo over him, it had taken seven

whole years for him to look at her without a strange pain tightening his chest.

In recent years, he had actually slept with her, explored her body and she had borne his child, and she expected that three measly years would heal his pain.

Since Cayman he was feeling vengeful. How dare the two of them look at him with pity and scorn in their eyes? Did they think that he was pathetic?

By the time he reached the house he was in a huff and slammed the front door. His mood was darker than ever. When he found Pinky Black in his study looking through his Thursday mail, a red mist surrounded his cornea.

"What are you doing?" he bellowed. She jumped, a frightened look in her eyes.

"I was expecting a letter." She had the manila envelop with his Cayman correspondence in her hands and a guilty expression on her face.

He advanced toward her and leaned his briefcase on his desk.

"Do not come into my study when I am not in here. Do not sort through my mail." He spoke slowly and deliberately and then snatched the mail from her nerveless fingers.

"Do you...do you spy on them?" Pinky whispered hoarsely.

"Get out of my study." Chris said fiercely.

"No." Pinky said defiantly. "You have been walking around here like a wounded animal all week. You are impossible to live with. So you had an affair with Kelly. So what? Why are you still so morose and dark and bitter? You are acting like she is the only woman in the world!"

Chris inhaled shakily and then sat down in his chair abruptly. "You have passed your place, Petrina."

He looked at her with hot fury emanating from his eyes.

Pinky recoiled from the look but held her ground. "You

need to hear the truth. You are acting as if she is the last woman on this planet. So what if she has a child for you? She does not want you in his life. She is happy with her husband. Couldn't you see that? Why can't you just let it go?" Pinky shouted. "Let it go and start living your life!"

Chris was so angry he could feel his heart hammering in his chest and a feeling of light-headedness taking him over.

He felt like lunging across the desk and ringing her neck—the nerve of this woman, talking to him like that. He looked at her trembling pink lips and out of the blue the random thought came to him that her lips were probably the reason she had the nickname Pinky. She was a pint-sized bundle of trouble, who needed to mind her own business.

"Petrina." He looked at her scornfully. "Get out of my study. Get out of my house. Get out of my life. Your antics, your outspokenness, I will not tolerate anymore. I will mail you a cheque for services already rendered. Now get out."

Pinky visibly quailed. "I won't apologize," she shouted, "and this time I am not coming back. You fire me every time I tell you the truth. I am fed up with you and your pity fest over Kelly."

She walked out of the study and slammed the door.

Chris swiveled around in his chair and faced the window outside. He was boiling mad.

So mad that he sat in the dark for hours trying to cool off. He had heard the front door slamming with force and then heard a car at the front.

Pinky was gone once again. He waited to feel the lightness that her departure would cause but the heaviness in his mood was still there.

He stayed in his chair until very late into the night, until finally he got up and headed to bed. He left the unopened manila envelope on his desk.

Chapter Five

The house was quiet on Friday morning when Chris got up from a troubled sleep. Usually, there was a cacophony of noise when Pinky was around. She sang loudly and effusively to her favorite gospel songs when she was in the shower and even in the sprawling six-bedroom house he could hear her down the hallway belting out some song or the other.

This morning the place was eerily quiet as if the life had been sucked out of it. Even Griffin, the multi-colored cat with a sash of white over his right eye was looking at him accusingly. He was waiting for Chris when he stepped out of the bedroom, he gave Chris a half hearted meow in greeting and headed toward Pinky's suite of rooms, standing at the door and looking back at Chris dejectedly.

"I can't believe this," Chris mumbled, "I am not going to let you and Pinky run my life."

Griffin still looked at him in feline accusation.

He kissed his teeth and headed toward Pinky's rooms. Last

time he had fired her, she had not taken all her things that had been an indication that she had intended to come back.

He pushed the door and Griffin ran ahead of him. The small sitting room was empty except for a gum wrapper on a side table. Her bedroom door was ajar and he pushed it open fully and was met with the sweet subtle smell of Pinky's perfume. She always smelled so good to him.

The spacious bedroom was devoid of all her belongings except for a textbook on the dresser and a picture of her stuck in its pages. She was using it as a bookmarker. He smiled to himself and drew it out.

There were several other pictures in the book too. He drew them out slowly and looked at them intently. There was one of her in a bathing suit with her brother Charles grinning in the camera. There was also one with her being held up in the arms of a muscular guy, who looked as if he was bench-pressing her. They were both grinning in the camera. She had in long gold braids and looked impossibly young and carefree.

He felt a slight twinge in his chest when he thought about how he shouted at her last night. He also felt a twinge of jealousy seeing her in the arms of the muscular guy.

He sighed and jammed the pictures back where he found them. The picture that he had dragged out first was on a chapter entitled Molecular Mechanics. He remembered her telling him that when she used her pictures as bookmarkers she associated the pictures to the topic she was studying. At the time he had thought she was crazy. But now he could see how it would work. Even though sometimes Pinky appeared scatterbrained and carefree, he could sense her intelligence and maturity. She just saw things from a different perspective than he did.

He ran his fingers through his hair and looked at Griffin

who was staring up at him a question in his eyes. Where is she?

"Probably at her brother's place in Flatbush." Chris said out loud to the cat.

Griffin jumped onto the bed and rubbed his head on Chris' hand.

"I am not going to be molly coddling you like Pinky," Chris said to a purring Griffin. "Pinky allows you to get away with too much."

He lay back on the bed and Griffin lay on top of him while he massaged his ears.

"And I won't ask her to come back either. You and I both know that this place didn't need a housekeeper in the first place. Pinky was just a huge distraction with her pert breasts and shapely bottom and her pinker than pink lips. Besides, whoever heard of a housekeeper with a pixie hair cut dyed in blonde and who could recite all the chemicals found in household polish, know their places on the periodic table and their reaction to each other? Pinky was no housekeeper."

Griffin meowed in ecstasy at the caress and Chris inhaled deeply. Pinky's scent was all over the room, like baby powder mixed with Pinky.

He sighed. He remembered the first time he had seen her, she was at Great Pond Church singing with a group of girls.

He had only stopped by that Wednesday night to drop off a package for a friend there. He had started avoiding the church since Estella, the girl he was dating, had revealed to Theo that he had been having an affair with Kelly, but that night he had made an unavoidable stop.

Surprisingly, from the group of eight girls, his eyes had zeroed in on Pinky—petite and pretty with a perky attitude that you could see on her face.

She hadn't seen him that night, but he knew she saw him

the day when she came for the interview. She had been tongue tied at first, but then that chirpy attitude had kicked in.

He could recall thinking—uncharitably—that he wanted her to keep working at Villa Rose for the duration of her studies just so he could see her everyday, but Meghan had come back and his mother had been hounding him to get a housekeeper.

On the spur of the moment he had hired Pinky and fired her a couple times since but somehow this felt final. Last night he had been furious and he was not in any mood to apologize. Pinky was not right for his peace of mind.

She made him feel...uneasy. Like a small pebble stuck in the corner of his shoe that he could not get out. Well, this time he pried her out and he was not letting her back in. He took one deep whiff of her scent again and stopped rubbing Griffin's head.

"Get up cat, it's just you me and Maud. Camille and Kenneth will be staying over for a few weeks so you'll have one more person to fawn over you since Camille likes cats. By the time they are gone we won't even remember that Pinky Black was here. I'll return her book today, because she probably needs it to study and then we are well rid of her."

Griffin blinked at him and meowed sorrowfully.

*****

"Why on earth are you crying?" Charles asked Pinky impatiently.

"Because I left my dratted book at his dratted place." Pinky hiccupped. She was in her Uncle's room. They both thought of it as the guest room because the place only had two bedrooms and her uncle hardly stayed at the house when he came anyway.

"You've been crying since I came to pick you up last night and I heard you sobbing away in here late into the night. You have the hots for Chris Donahue, admit it. That's the first step out of addiction Pinky—admitting you have a problem."

"Shut up," Pinky said wiping her eyes, "I have an exam in five days, I need that book."

Charles leaned on the doorjamb. "Talk to Uncle Charles, I was recently heart broken I can relate."

"You didn't love Phoebe," Pinky snorted, "you had a crush on her because she is gorgeous. If you had loved Phoebe you would not have moved on so quickly with Tanya."

"Ah." Charles moved from the doorjamb and sat on the bed. "So you love him. You don't just have a crush on him because he's gorgeous?"

"Argh," Pinky growled, "you are something else."

"So what happened?" Charles asked. "Last night I could barely get two words out of you. I thought he had beaten you or something the way you were wailing when you got into the car."

"He doesn't like me like that," Pinky said forlornly, "he loves Kelly Palmer. Remember at Phoebe's wedding you saw this lady with curly hair at the front; she was in this nice swirly halter neck dress. Her husband did the ceremony."

Charles nodded. "That's Erica's sister. She's really nice— really nice."

He grinned.

"She's not that nice," Pinky said scornfully, "I saw two strands of silver hair in her lustrous curls. Two." She held up her fingers scornfully.

Charles laughed. "That's it? That's all the criticism you can find for her? I have more than two strands of silver hair on my head and I'm only twenty-five."

Pinky sighed, "I've been trying to find something wrong with her physically but I can't. And I mean I've tried hard."

"So what if he loves her?" Charles shrugged. "The woman is married and looks happy to me. You should have seen her and the husband dancing closely at the reception. It's a good thing Chris didn't stay for that or he would have had a seizure. They were looking in each others eyes and he was whispering sweet nothings in her ear."

"They had an affair," Pinky said smirking, "he slept with her, knocked her up, the last child is Chris'."

Charles frowned. "You don't have to sound so gleeful when you say it. This whole situation must be tough on them."

Pinky slumped her shoulders. "Sorry, I know I shouldn't be feeling resentful towards Kelly but she should have known better than to have an affair and encourage Chris."

"They are both adults."

"I know. I know. It's just that she's my love rival," Pinky said to Charles pettishly. "She has my man's affections."

Charles laughed. "You mean your boss' affections."

"That's right, my boss and only my boss. He's a boss by the book, only tolerating me like I'm an employee. If he could have an affair with her, why can't he make even a slight pass at me?" Pinky asked plaintively. "Why can't he leer at me…act all sleazy and repulsive…treat me like a thing… slap my ass when I pass by? Why is he so gentlemanly, and standoffish, and cold?"

"Because you are an ugly troll," Charles said grinning, "and he has to prove to you that not all men are animals with sex at the forefront of their minds."

Pinky threw a pillow at him. "I am serious, if he lost all control over Kelly, a married woman, why can't he lose control over me. Love me. What is it about that one woman that has him so darned fixated? Argh…argh…argh…" she banged her head on the wall.

"Do I need to be super-sexy? Do I need to be married to a pastor?"

Charles cleared his throat. "It's simple, Pinky."

"It is?" Pinky asked looking at her brother with avid curiosity.

"You just have to be his first love, but that first love seems to be Kelly," Charles said. "Some men never ever get over their first love. They function in other relationships but their first love holds the key to their heart. They'll ditch their current women with a million and one kids if their first love crooks a little finger and says I'm available. The problem here is that Kelly was Chris' first love; I am thinking Theo must have been Kelly's so she stuck with him."

"That's rubbish!" Pinky gasped. "People move on from that sort of thing. Time generally takes care of that."

"Nope," Charles said contemplatively, "this first love theory thing has merit. Especially if you haven't lived with a person and gotten to know their faults and their quirks and all the other boring stuff, then they will be forever in your mind as the ideal. I think that's what your boss is going through."

"But they had sex and got to experience the forbidden," Pinky whispered, "the mystery was solved for both of them, there was no more need to wonder what if."

"The sex part made it worse." Charles got up. "It showed him what he was missing. And to make it worse she has his baby. I think you should forget about Chris Donahue, he's not a good option for you right now. He is badly damaged goods. You'll always be second best to him."

Pinky looked at Charles with a scared look in her eyes, "but he's my first love. Am I going to be damaged goods to any man after this?"

"No," Charles grinned, "you'll get over it. You can stop

the cancer of emotion from spreading and set your life right now. One day you'll find a guy and wonder why on earth you were so hung up on Chris Donahue. In the meantime, want me to run up to his place and get your book."

Pinky opened her mouth and then closed it. "I...I...could just call..."

"Addicted," Charles said shaking his head.

"Who died and made you relationship guru?" Pinky asked bitterly.

"I have seen a lot my child." Charles scratched his goatee. "I am thinking of dying my goatee blond like your hair, what do you think?"

Before Pinky could answer her cell phone rang. She picked it up absentmindedly,

"Hello."

"You left your textbook," Chris said to her. "I have it at my office. Want me to drop it off somewhere later?"

"Er..." Pinky looked at Charles in panic, "I... er..."

"I just thought of this," Chris said ignoring her stammering. "Caleb is trying out some new dishes. You can come by and try them out with me at lunch."

He hung up before she could say no. She stared at her phone bemused.

"Oh boy," Charles said leaving the room. "Unfortunately, I am going to have to leave you and your love life for a while. I am going to be staying at the hotel for the next couple of weeks, management training plus my job. This is the busy season you know."

"So aren't you going home for the Christmas holiday?" Pinky asked. Their parents lived in deep rural Hanover. Christmas there was usually a traditional event filled with traditional Jamaican dishes, extended family and lots of laughter.

"No, don't think so," Charles said sorrowfully, "maybe only Christmas day. I want to be one of the four management trainees chosen from the program."

"I guess I'll find my way there then," Pinky said, "alone."

"I'll talk to you later," Charles said hurrying out. "Remember that Chris Donahue is damaged, so handle with care."

Pinky pondered the things that Charles had said. He had a point. Chris was damaged goods and she would forever be second best. She looked at her suitcases and contemplated whether she should unpack them.

Chapter Six

When Pinky arrived at Villa Rose, Meghan waved to her. "Hey, Girl."

"Hi Megs, I am here to see Mr. Donahue."

"He said you should go right into the conference room." Meghan smiled. "And may I say, your shoes look fabulous."

Pinky looked down at herself. She was dressed in a bronze Onesie short suit that closely matched her complexion and a pair of multicolored wedge sandals that she had picked up at a craft fair from a Rastafarian man who did them as a hobby.

"It's custom made." She laughed at Meghan. "Go down to the craft village and ask for Fitzroy, tell him that Pinky sent you."

"Okay, definitely will—thanks." Meghan smiled at her.

Pinky inhaled sharply and walked to the conference room. The first thing that hit her when she opened the door was the scent of delicious food.

Caleb was in there with Chris. The two men looked up when she walked in and Caleb whistled, "pretty girl." He winked at her good-naturedly.

"Hello gentlemen." She sat down at the far end of the table, barely glancing at Chris.

"Hello lady," Chris said half seriously. "Caleb is changing up his menu for Christmas, so I thought you'd like to have samples with us today."

"The three of us?" Pinky asked.

"Sure," Chris said nonchalantly, "that's if you don't have anything else to do."

"Are you going to apologize to me for your behavior last night?" Pinky asked, finally looking at him fully.

It was a mistake. He looked even better than he did yesterday. He was in a grey suit and a crisp white shirt; as usual he didn't have on a tie. His hair was slicked back from his forehead in curly waves and his jaw looked clean-shaven. Those hazel eyes of his were watching her with growing incredulity.

"Well?" He flexed his fingers. "I wasn't in the best of moods, I'm sorry for my behavior."

"Good." Pinky nodded and got up.

She moved closer to Chris and Caleb around the table. "What is this you have here Caleb?"

Caleb was watching her and Chris with a bemused look on his face.

"Ehem, well, I...are you two dating or something?"

"No," both Chris and Pinky said at the same time.

"I was his housekeeper," Pinky said. "He fired me last night."

Caleb nodded and opened the first covered dish. "This is a sample of the several hors d'oeuvres that will be served to our guests. Please feel free to criticize."

He watched the two of them for a while. "So why did Chris fire you?"

"Because he is paranoid," Pinky said quickly before Chris could reply.

Chris held up his hand. "I don't think Pinky and I are a good fit."

Caleb's eyebrow shot up on his forehead.

"Employment wise," Chris said quickly.

"Anyway," Pinky said morosely, "he is still in love with your sister-in-law. And anybody else is surplus to requirements."

"This is an ackee puff pastry," Caleb said quickly before Chris could respond.

"Asking you to lunch was a bad idea," Chris said hoarsely. "I am sorry if I've ever given you the idea that there is any hope for a deeper relationship between us."

Caleb got up quickly. "I shouldn't be hearing this. This is private talk. I could come back when this is sorted out."

Pinky and Chris ignored him—staring at each other hotly. Chris only looked away from Pinky when the door made a click as Caleb made his exit.

Pinky snorted, "let it all out Mr. Donahue, I'm not in your employ anymore. You can't fire me again just for knowing that you spy on Kelly Palmer and that you get a report on her and your child every Thursday."

Chris got up and looked through the conference window turning his back to her. Even here, the place had a nice view of the rose gardens and the sea.

He sighed, a deep heartfelt sigh, he could see her reflection in the glass, his little pint sized terror in a bronze shorts suit and her blonde hair. He had been very happy when she actually stepped into the conference room; he had missed her this morning, he hadn't realized how accustomed he had gotten to inane chatter before he came to work.

He spun around to face her. "I missed you this morning."

Pinky gasped. "You did?" Her brown eyes lit up with joy and then she slumped back in the chair. "It's easy to get used to anybody and miss them when they are no longer around."

Chris grinned. "But Griffin and I agreed that you are just not anybody."

Pinky smiled. "I am not going to let you turn my head with your compliments, and I'm not going to come back to work for you either. You are too depressed and serious and damaged."

Chris frowned. "I'm damaged aren't I?"

He nodded contemplatively and then looked at her fully. "I don't spy on Kelly Palmer. I spy on my child. I made Theo a promise that I would stay away from his family, and technically I have. But I am not the kind of guy who can forget that he has an offspring in the world. So I have a detective give me a weekly report. I hope you can appreciate that I am not only depressed when I get that report. It also reminds me, once more, that I was weak, I went against all the known principles that I had held, and that I had an affair with a married woman."

"Have you asked God for forgiveness?" Pinky asked him earnestly, "You are acting as if God can't forgive you this sin and you have to keep reminding yourself about how bad you were. If for one minute you decide to let it go and let God, what do you think will happen? You are going to feel again. You are going to join the land of the living again, but you are afraid."

"So when are your exams?" Chris asked abruptly.

"That's it, you are just going to change the topic?" Pinky shook her head exasperatedly. "Next week Monday, I have two on Wednesday and two on Friday. Then I am done. I may go home after, Charles won't be around and I don't have anything to hang around for."

She glanced at Chris and then looked away. "I expect you'll be busy with your sisters coming and all."

Chris nodded. "It usually is a blast. Family means everything to the Donahues."

"My family has a really nice thing too. Charles will only be coming for Christmas Day but my cousin Hal is bringing his friend Lance from Kingston, and they are spending the whole week. I used to have a crush on Lance when I was younger. He was just so..."

"Stop." Chris shook his head. "Do you want us to keep sampling these dishes or what?"

"Sample the dishes of course." Pinky smiled slyly.

Chris was looking bothered and jittery after he heard about Lance and that was a balm to her sore ego.

Chapter Seven

"Chris, can you look anymore depressed?" Camille sat beside him with a cup of chocolate in her hand.

His brother-in-law Kenneth whistled. "I second that."

Camille looked at her husband contemplatively. "Since he came to pick us up from the airport, three days ago, he's been giving us fake smiles and forced laughter."

Hyacinth Donahue joined them in the living room with a tray of teacups in her hands. "I don't know what has gotten into him. It's Christmas Eve, look lively, your nieces and nephews are here. It's family time." Then a cloud passed over her face. "Sorry Chris."

Chris looked at all three of them resignedly. "Sorry about what?"

"Sorry for being so insensitive." Hyacinth sighed. "I forgot that not all the family is here."

"Oh," Camille said sadly, "he's thinking about Mark. My

adorable and totally sweet nephew that is growing up with the wrong name."

Chris shrugged, "I wasn't thinking about Mark." He heaved himself from the settee that he had dropped into since arriving at his parent's house. His father had taken the rest of the family to a pre-Christmas party; Camille and Kenneth had not wanted to go.

"I wasn't thinking about anything." He justified his lie inwardly, you couldn't call Pinky an anything.

He hadn't seen or heard from her in two weeks. He had deliberately not called her during her exams, and when he tried calling after her exams were finished, she ignored his calls. Though he wanted to deny it, he was missing her dreadfully, more dreadfully than he could account for. On all her exam days he had prayed that she was successful. When her exams were over he found himself wanting to dial her number and ask her out.

For the first time in years he was fully tied up in his mind with someone other than Kelly. Though the feeling had been frightening, he had gotten used to it this past week. Then he remembered that she had spoken of some guy named Lance who was supposed to be spending all Christmas with her and that she had had a crush on him—then the thought entered his head that he must do something about it.

Pinky was a smart and intelligent girl; any man in his right mind would snatch her up. He couldn't afford for this Lance fellow to be acting on her old crush and taking advantage of her. A man had to protect his former housekeeper to the best of his ability.

Hyacinth came and wrapped her arms around Chris. "Darling, I have been talking to a daughter of an old friend of mine."

Chris looked down at his mother's upturned face dazedly.

"Huh?"

"About the whole Mark issue," Hyacinth said. "She said that you may be able to get shared custody of Mark, if you really wanted to."

"What?" Chris finally focused his mind on what his mother was saying. "I could?"

"Yes." Hyacinth nodded excitedly. "She was explaining all the legal mumbo jumbo but I told her she would have to explain it to you first hand."

"Is that so?" Camille piped up. "I think you should talk to her Chris, the arrangement with the Palmers really leaves you out in the cold. It is unfair of them. Why should you have to be the one to lose out on seeing your own flesh and blood just because they dictated it as so?"

"But," Chris massaged the back of his neck absentmindedly, "I promised Theo I would stay a way. They are happy. I saw them in Cayman the other day at Phoebe's wedding. If I step in now it would cause them extra pain."

Kenneth who was silent until then, chirped in, "if it ain't broke, don't fix it."

"How can you say that?" Camille turned to her husband. "Having your own child is the most precious thing."

"No it's not," Kenneth said exasperatedly, "this is not about Chris alone. This is about a family moving on from an infidelity and doing it the best way they know how. For Chris to interfere now is ungodly."

"To separate me from my grandson is ungodly," Hyacinth said hotly.

"And besides they have two others," Camille said turning to Kenneth, "they should be satisfied with that."

"Lord help you." Kenneth laughed. "Children are not like toys, you have two so the third one shouldn't matter? They are human beings who you bond with. Now despite the fact that I think Theo is a saint for taking back Kelly, he has already bonded with the child and if he should have to share custody with another man, the man who knocked up his wife, then that's a whole other ball game. You were thinking of us adopting." Kenneth looked at Camille sharply. "Would it be okay if we just sent back whichever kid they gave us because of some problem or the other?"

Camille shook her head. "No it wouldn't be, it's just that I have been trying for years to get pregnant. Both of us are okay, we did the tests and everything." She glanced at her mother. " Suppose this is Chris' only chance to have a child. He'll be losing out to Theo."

"He'll live," Kenneth said looking at Chris contemplatively. "There are plenty of men who don't have kids or can't have any. Your obsession with your situation is clouding the issue. I will live too honey, if we don't have any. Marie and Fiona have enough children between the two of them to satisfy Harlan and Hyacinth."

He gave Hyacinth a sharp look. "Leave Chris alone with this situation, encouraging him to pursue this matter will only hurt the other family."

Hyacinth sat daintily, "I think Chris is being unfairly treated and an injustice has to be corrected."

Kenneth looked at Chris who had walked over to the windows and had his back to them. "Do you have anything to say about this?"

"It can't hurt to hear what my options are," Chris said shrugging, "I love my son, I get a weekly report on him every Thursday." He slumped his shoulders. "Some Thursdays I think that the weekly report is not enough."

Hyacinth smiled in relief. "I'll ask Geraldine to come over and explain the legalities to you dear and then you can make up your mind."

Chris frowned. "What time is it?"

Hyacinth glanced at her watch. "Nine o' clock. Why?"

"I am going to Hanover tomorrow," Chris said determinedly. "I need to go home and catch some shut eye."

"Tomorrow is Christmas!" Hyacinth said alarmed, "what business is there to do on Christmas Day?"

Chris shrugged. "I just have to see if Pinky is fine. Her family lives in Hanover."

"Pinky?" the three of them looked at him with varying degrees of alarm.

"My housekeeper," Chris said smiling. "She did her exam last week, I haven't heard from her all week. I need to go check that she's okay."

"That girl is not a proper housekeeper," Hyacinth said in disgust, "she's too brash and sure of herself. Why don't you just call her?"

Camille laughed. "Welcome to the land of the living Christopher Donahue. Go and make sure that Pinky is fine. When can I meet her? I don't care how brash and sure of herself she is. I love her already."

"Well," Chris said shrugging on his jacket, "she's not my housekeeper anymore, I sort of fired her last time we had a quarrel."

"Good," Hyacinth said, "she dresses outrageously and dyes her hair platinum blonde. Not presentable at all. I'll find you a nice housekeeper dear."

Kenneth cleared his throat. "Mother, I think that Chris is fine with this particular housekeeper." He winked at Chris. "Now we know the reason for the bad mood."

Chris grimaced. "It's not like that at all."

"Denial, denial." Camille shook her head. "We'll miss you tomorrow but we are going to be here for three more weeks, so no biggie."

"Okay, later guys." Chris left the house and Hyacinth sat there puzzled.

"Are you telling me that that creature who looks like she could be the centerfold of a dirty magazine is who my son is interested in?"

Camille nodded delightfully. "Yes, I can't wait to meet her."

Chapter Eight

It was drizzling slightly when Chris set out for Hanover. He had called Charles in the night and Charles had reluctantly given him directions. Chris had no idea why he was even going to what sounded like the most rural part of Jamaica on Christmas Day.

Pinky was not answering her phone and there was that niggling feeling that she was planning to flirt with this Lance fellow who she had a crush on in the past.

His irrational possessiveness toward Pinky was bordering on the ridiculous, but he couldn't help it. He turned on the car radio but there were just too many Christmas carols—station after station—he wasn't feeling particularly festive and he was not in the mood to hear them.

He pushed a CD into the player without looking at it and the first song was Ordinary People by John Legend. He slowed down his speed considerably and instantly he thought about Kelly. This was their mutually loved song.

Usually when he heard it, he got into a depression so severe he had to wonder if he would survive it, but today was different. He couldn't place what it was. Since seeing her in person in Cayman, the intensity that he felt for her wasn't there anymore.

Perversely, that had made him depressed, the feeling that he had for Kelly was something that he had carried around for so long that he felt as if it was a part of him. Now it was just a shadow of what it was. There were times when he actually found himself struggling to remember the intensity of it.

He rehashed his memories with her, but the tinge of pain that he usually felt was absent. Like the first moment they actually spoke, he had felt unusually shy around her. He wasn't a shy person but he could recall her sitting in her parents' sofa, her brown eyes bright and inquisitive listening to him speak.

Lola, her mother, had approached him about her wayward daughter who needed a bit of nudging to come to church. He didn't know what to expect, but when he went to speak to who he believed would be a rebellious child, he found an attractive and intelligent woman who was quite open to visiting church.

He had left that day determined to see more of her, and he had. He dated her for close to six months before they kissed. They had been on a rafting tour on the blue Lagoon, it was a cloudless night with the lights from the surrounding villas reflecting off the water and creating a romantic ambience. There was a gentle breeze, he had leaned into her and kissed her.

He had never forgotten how that kiss felt. It had cemented his feelings for her. He had made up his mind that she was the one, the only woman for him. He had an elaborate proposal destination picked out; he had even bought an expensive property on Bluffs Head where they could build their house together.

He had thoroughly planned their life together, not realizing that Kelly had been torn in her emotions. He had been so confident in their mutual compatibility that he had actually treated her outings with the pastor as non-threatening.

After all, Theo was poor competition for him. Theo had just started his career in the clergy, whilst he had been working in his family property development business for a few years and had become an established wheeler and dealer by then. Chris' certainty that Kelly would see him as a good catch made him blasé about her regular outings with the pastor.

He had found her hiking trip to the Blue Mountains to be a cute little outing that he was too busy to attend. He had never really understood her fascination with nature walks and hiking. He should have gotten it because that was the one thing that sealed his doom.

He turned the car into a dusty, narrow track that was full of ruts, there were trees overhanging the path and he could hear some of them scraping the top of his SUV. What if Charles had given him wrong directions? He had certainly sounded grumpy earlier on the phone, like he was half annoyed or half asleep.

At least he hadn't asked why Chris was interested in learning where his parents lived so late in the night.

Chris' mind wandered back to Kelly and his heartbreak. She had called him when he was in the middle of a meeting and sounding unusually subdued, announced that she was getting married to Theo Palmer, the junior pastor at the church. He had thought she was joking and he had told her that the joke was in poor taste. She had gone silent on the phone and then sighed. His heart had raced, a sharp jump that had him clutching his chest. He had slumped on the wall, the cell phone clutched to his ear.

He didn't remember a word that she had said after that. Apparently his father had found him crouched on the floor outside the conference room and called a doctor. He had never really told Kelly how she had given him the shock of his life.

The pain after that had come in fits and spurts. Some days he was all right and some days he felt so broken inside that he couldn't get up out of bed. He hadn't realized how invested in Kelly he had been.

He had thrown the invitation to their wedding in his waste paper basket then carried the basket outside and lit the whole thing on fire. He had also developed some bad habits, like driving like a crazy man on the road everyday, hoping that someone would hit him from the road.

Then he had gradually gotten over Kelly. Bit by bit, the pain had subsided. Then he could look at her in church, even when she was pregnant with her children for Theo and not feel a thing.

When she started working for him, she had looked unhappy and he had offered her a listening ear, and then one day talking had turned into touching and then full on sex. He had found himself in the unenviable position of being the other man.

He winced inwardly. He hadn't been comfortable facing Theo during a board meeting at church, knowing that he was having sex with his wife. He had even started rationalizing it, thinking that he should be the one that she was married to, and not Theo—so all was well with the world. And then, once more Kelly had chosen Theo. Except this time she had been pregnant with his child.

He pulled up near a house at the end of the track and

suddenly realized what he had done. He had come all the way to Hanover to see Pinky Black on a family holiday, when he should have been with his family.

He looked over at the modest house painted in white and surrounded by flowers and then on the dashboard clock. It was six-thirty in the morning. There was no sign of life at the house.

If he drove back to St. Ann now he could reach back at his parent's house by eight-thirty. He sat back in his seat and thought about just turning back. He was acting strange even to himself. There was no rhyme or reason why he should be here at this time.

He looked behind when he heard a car pull up behind his. It was Charles Black.

He stretched and came over to the side of Chris' vehicle. "Don't tell me you reached here before me."

Chris wound down his window. "It seems as if I did."

"Well come on in then," Charles said. "They should have been up a long time ago. These are late hours for country people you know."

Charles started bellowing. "Moms, Pops."

The front door cracked open and Pinky came out.

"You made it Charlie Charles." She was in a skimpy pair of khaki shorts, showing off her perfect legs and an orange tube top with a sliver of her belly showing. She had her hair in fine blonde braids, which hung to her hips. Chris slowly ran his eyes over her and then his eyes collided with her shocked ones.

"What are you doing here?" Pinky asked wiping her eyes.

She looked at Charles who was grinning beside her. "Do you see Chris Donahue over there, or did the Chemistry exam scramble my brain?"

"He's over there," Charles said grinning. "I guess this

whole love thing isn't as one-sided as you reported."

Pinky snorted. "It is. Trust me."

"Hello Mr. Donahue." She slowly walked up to where Chris was standing with uncertainty in every step. He was in a navy blue shirt and blue jeans, he had his hands thrust in his pocket and he had a puzzled look on his face.

"Hello, Miss Black," he answered gruffly. "How many bedrooms are in this house?"

"Three," Pinky said slowly and looking at him curiously.

"So where did Lance sleep?" Chris asked his hazel eyes fixed on her.

Pinky chuckled and answered sarcastically. "With me of course. The nights are very chilly now you know. A warm body is very welcomed."

Chris frowned. "Seriously?"

Pinky threw up her hands in the air. "What are you doing here?"

"I came to check up on you, " Chris said slowly, his head snapped up when a bare-chested guy stepped out on the veranda rubbing his eyes blearily.

"Where's my Pinkylicious, we were in the middle of something."

Pinky sighed. "Over here Lance."

Chris stiffened and glared at Lance hostilely. "I can't believe that you are carrying on like this in your parents' house."

"They endorsed it," Pinky said cheekily, "my mother even insisted on it."

Chris gasped. "You told me they were good Christian folks."

"They are," Pinky said grinning, "but every year at this time they allow me to do it."

"Hey," Lance waved to Chris, "are you coming to join us?"

"What?" Chris asked confused.

Lance sighed. "The rubbing of the cake. Aunt Sophia has all of us taking turns. This year she shared out the cake to everybody and left none for the family, so we are baking on Christmas Day. You are Pinky's Chris?"

Pinky was gesticulating behind Chris' back wildly. "Don't tell him anything." She was jumping up and down and mouthing to Lance vociferously but he ignored her.

Chris smiled slowly. "She told you about me?"

Lance nodded. "You are all she's going on and on about all week. The whole house is sick and tired of hearing about you."

Pinky sighed dejectedly. "This is going to be one Christmas."

Chris looked at her and smiled softly. "Oh yes it is."

*****

Pinky's parents were jovial folks. Her mother loved to cook and every opportunity she got she told stories about the various dishes she had made through the years. Pinky's father was just starting out into rearing livestock and he had several tales to tell about his new venture. They treated him like they had always known him, as if he had been invited for the holidays. He began to see where Pinky and Charles got their people skills from, he felt relaxed and part of the Black family in a matter of seconds.

The kitchen was a flurry of activity. Lance and Pinky were mixing butter and sugar together when he went in. He was feeling a little awkward but after the introductions Pinky's mother, Sofia, gave him an identical smile to her daughter's, declared him a fine looking young man and handed him a wooden spoon and a pan of batter.

She was an older version of Pinky; they even had in the same blonde braids—she was a little rounder, but she looked much younger than he had imagined.

Her father was just as effusive; he was a big muscular man, almost as tall as Chris and sported an eye patch. He came in from the fields with a big bunch of plantains and proceeded to make breakfast, all the while commenting on his farming activities. He made some large flour dumplings with ackee and saltfish and strong chocolate tea from cocoa that they had growing in their back yard.

They had breakfast on the back veranda with Charles moaning about his newest managerial venture.

"That girl Phoebe really lit a fire under your ambition," Peter Black said laughing. "I like it. How did it feel going to her wedding?"

"It was cool," Charles said grinning. "She looked really pretty but Tanya was just as gorgeous."

"Tell me more about Tanya," Sofia said coming around the table. "Why can't we meet her yet?"

"Her mother has a young baby, they are big on Christmas too, so I couldn't get her to tear herself away," Charles said fondly.

Sofia looked at Chris a pleasant look in her eyes. "So how long are you staying?"

Chris was surprised; he had no idea he would have been so easily accepted by the family, they were even asking him how long he was staying. "Well, I only came for the day."

Both Sofia and Peter nodded. "You are welcome."

Chris nodded back and then glanced at a blushing Pinky. What had she been telling her parents about him? Lance had said she talked about him all week.

He looked over at Lance who was tucking into his breakfast like a starving man. He didn't appear as if he cared one way or another that Pinky had a male friend coming to visit.

Chris concluded that Pinky had been putting him on about Lance. He reluctantly conceded that Pinky knew just how to make him jealous and she exploited it constantly.

But why was he so jealous and possessive over her though? It's not as if he loved her. He stopped staring at her long enough to get back in his breakfast.

*****

Christmas at the Black's was loud, boisterous and full of laughs. Chris found himself on more than one occasion guffawing with the rest of them. They had roped him into playing dominoes and helping out in the kitchen at intervals. He barely found himself alone with Pinky; the place was just so busy.

Every few minutes a community member would stop by and they would have a relaxed talk and laugh with whoever it was. They would introduce him as Pinky's friend.

Pinky's cousin, Hal, came by in the mid-day with his parents and his girlfriend. His girlfriend, Sherifah, was studying law at Harvard; she kept seeking out Chris and smiling at him brightly.

Pinky was watching Sherifah closely and when she cornered Chris on the veranda, she went out and said loudly, "Sherifah, your dainty hands are needed in the kitchen."

Sherifah looked up resentfully, she was just about to engage Chris in conversation.

She got up with a huff. "I'll soon be back Chris."

"She has a crush," Lance said grinning." Hal needs to rein that girl in, but if he doesn't Pinky will."

They had finished helping Sofia with vegetables in the kitchen and were sitting on the back veranda.

Lance had a glass of sorrel in his hand. "Pinky has been trying to avoid you, but since you arrived she has lit up like a Christmas tree."

Chris had to smile at that.

The back veranda had several lounge chairs on it and overlooked rolling hills in the distance and a plantain grove just below the house—all the trees had bunches of fruit on them.

"I love this place," Lance said sighing. "I started coming here with Hal from college days."

He laughed, a hint of nostalgia in his voice. "Pinky was a skinny little thing with bright pink pouting lips who wanted to follow us everywhere."

Chris looked at him assessingly. "Do you like her?"

"Of course," Lance said shaking his head. "I love my little Pinky, but as a sister... I love the whole family. I am closer to them than my own. I think of myself as the honorary nephew. I stay with them rather than with Hal when I come to this part of the world."

Chris exhaled. "That's a relief."

Lance guffawed, "I knew it would be, that's why I am telling you this to put you out of your misery."

Chris protested. "It's not like that with Pinky and me. We are friends, I think."

Lance laughed again. "This is too funny. I haven't played pretend since I was around nine."

Chris grunted uncomfortably. "I am going to get some sorrel."

*****

Dinner was a lively affair, filled with several dishes, each one seeming to outdo the next. The dining table could only seat eight persons, so Chris followed Pinky under an almond tree where there were tables and chairs arranged for the spill over of people.

"I can't believe I am having Christmas dinner with you," Pinky said wonderingly, "it's surreal."

Chris shrugged. "It's not that big of a deal."

"Don't your folks celebrate Christmas?" she asked with a smirk.

"Yes," Chris said, "they make a big production of it."

"Yet here you are," Pinky said triumphantly. "I feel special."

"You weren't answering your phone," Chris shrugged, "had to make sure you were alright. How were your exams?" he asked hurriedly.

Pinky looked as if she was going to dance on the table from excitement.

"Good," she said enthusiastically, "I was moping over my boss but I think I got the questions right. Just three more months of school to go and then I am done.

"So what's next after that?" Chris asked, he had never really thought about that before, Pinky could decide to move away from the St. Ann area. He'd never see her. That filled him with sudden dread.

"Next." Pinky thought about it and then looked up in the air. "I'll get married to a gorgeous hunk and have two children with very high IQ's."

"Are you serious?" Chris asked her alarmed. Did she have somebody she was planning to marry? One never knew with Pinky.

Pinky smiled softly. "No, just wishful thinking. I think I'm going to do my masters in forensic science, or apply for medical school, or set up a lab at home and make perfume, or," she snapped her fingers, "I could do environmental law or write a science thriller. The possibilities are endless with chemistry. I could basically work in any industry I feel like. Chemistry is a very versatile science. Students of chemistry are supposed to be able to solve problems and think things through, so the area is wide open."

Chris nodded while staring at her animated face; while she was talking he had this urge to kiss her.

"But anyway," Pinky said eating her food again, "I wouldn't mind doing something that is life changing preferably in the cosmetic industry. Maybe find a new formula to make hair dye that isn't harmful to the skin or find a way to make hair relaxers without using harsh ingredients."

Chris smiled. "For that you'd need your own lab at home. Coincidentally I have a big part of my basement that would be perfect for that."

Pinky frowned at his last statement but declined to say anything about it.

Chris finished eating and leaned back in his chair, some family friends had started playing dominoes at a table in the distance. He glanced at his watch. "I am going to leave shortly. I want to catch a little piece of the Christmas with my family."

Pinky nodded. "I am so overwhelmed that you came today. I don't know what to think about you now."

"Well," Chris scratched his chin, "you could come back to work for me in the New Year. I promise I won't fire you for the rest of the time you are there."

Pinky shifted in her seat uncomfortably. "Chris I don't know if you know this," she lowered her voice, "but I have a thing for you, working at your place is not going to help it go away. You love somebody else and you are emotionally unavailable and I'm not going to be waiting around for you to take fifty years to get over her so that I can have a chance. So, I am going to have to a pass on your offer. Maybe I can find a job somewhere else where I am not emotionally invested in my boss."

Chris stared at her stunned; he never expected her to be so blunt about her feelings and refuse his job offer. "Are you saying that you will not work for me unless I love you or something like that?"

"You got it." Pinky said standing up and stacking up their plates. "I love you. Some days I hate you but most times I love you. I am weak with it and I am not going to work for you so that I can get more embroiled in you and your damageness."

"Damageness is not even a word," Chris said getting up too. He followed her through to the kitchen and watched as she scraped together the excess food into a container. "Pinky." She looked up at him sadly, her pink lips trembling. He sighed and ran his fingers through his hair. His curls were too low for it to have any effect but he still continued the gesture. "How did emotions like love get into this?"

Pinky shrugged, "I don't know, I am usually a logical thinker. This whole love thing has blindsided me."

He leaned forward and gave her a hard kiss on her lips. "I'll call you. Answer my calls okay."

"Okay," Pinky whispered, touching her lips in awe. She watched his retreating back and leaned up on the counter weakly.

Chapter Nine

When Chris arrived home from his parent's house on Christmas night he was feeling extremely sleepy.

His mother had pressed a business card into his hand. "Geraldine Brown, Attorney-at-law. She is expecting your call at the end of the month," Hyacinth had said with a hopeful look in her eyes. "I think it's a good way to start the New Year—sorting out this whole mess in your favor."

He had left the card on the desk in his study. He wasn't sure that it was great way to start the New Year.

He was torn. If he made that call, he would be starting the wheels in motion to get access to his son, to maybe exact some revenge on Kelly.

He couldn't deny that when he saw her at Phoebe's wedding that her plaintive cry of, "why can't you move on?" had made him angry. She and Theo had no right to look at him like that.

He felt like punishing them both. He was not the only one

who had been involved in their sordid little triangle but he was the only one being punished. But then, he thought about Mark. He was a happy well-adjusted child. If he truly loved him he would leave him alone or would he?

Shouldn't a child grow up knowing his roots? He couldn't imagine not knowing who his real father was. Harlan had been present in all aspects of his life. His father had set a sterling example of what it meant to be a responsible man and a family man.

He pondered his options for the whole holiday period. He had several debates about it with Camille and Kenneth. Camille was all for him trying to get Mark but Kenneth told him to leave it alone.

He called Pinky occasionally and found himself depending on the phone calls to brighten his day. He didn't say a word to her about his current dilemma. He didn't dare. Pinky would tell him to just snap out of it and move on.

He often wondered why he found Pinky, with her casual attitude and plain speaking, so attractive. He wasn't sure how he really felt about her; all he knew was that when she wasn't around he missed her and that she brought out really extreme emotions from him—like anger and jealousy. He could not recall feeling such a range of extremes before.

He tapped his hand on his desk and glanced at the card surreptitiously. Should he or shouldn't he?

He picked up his cell phone and dialed the number, almost reluctantly.

"Geraldine Brown speaking," a snappy business-like voice said over the phone.

"Oh, hi Geraldine, Christopher Donahue here. Are you free anytime today?"

"Christopher Donahue," Geraldine said laughing softly, her snappy business-like attitude forgotten. "I bet you don't remember little Gerry with those infernal pig tails and those hideous braces I used to wear."

"No I don't remember," Chris said warmly, "so are you free today?"

"I am free right now," Geraldine purred. "I am once more single and disengaged. My divorce became final today."

"I... er." Chris was puzzled. "Didn't my mother tell you about my situation? She said you could help."

"Oh!" Geraldine laughed uncomfortably. "Your mother and I spoke about many things; one of them was that you were single and wanting to mingle."

Chris cleared his throat. "Well I was calling about that little issue of my son. Not the single thing."

"Bummer," Geraldine said grumpily, "I was hoping you were calling to comfort my recently divorced heart. That's why I told your Mom December 31 you know."

"Well," Chris leaned back in his chair, "if it's not convenient to discuss the legal issue, I can understand."

"No—no," Geraldine said quickly, "give me directions to your place and I'll be up there as soon as possible."

Chris hurriedly gave her directions and when he hung up the persistent thought that this was not going to be such a good idea came back to haunt him.

*****

Geraldine arrived at the house an hour later. Chris was in his study and Maud showed her through. He looked up from the computer and got up hurriedly.

"Geraldine Brown, you look great." He smiled at her genuinely.

Geraldine was tall almost as tall as he was. She had long thick black hair, which she wore in a ponytail and a roundish face that highlighted her mixed Asian parentage and slanted eyes that shone with intelligence. She wore a bright burgundy lipstick that matched her business suit, which fit her slim frame neatly.

He could vaguely remember her now. She was one of four or five little brats who his mother used to baby-sit on those rare occasions when her parents couldn't pick them up from school.

Geraldine smiled at Chris easily. "And you look handsome, as I am sure you know."

"Can I offer you anything?" Chris asked her before he sat down, "juice, water, food?"

"No," Geraldine shuddered, "I am on a strict diet, imbibed too much of my mother's food over the holiday. My parents were compensating for my heartbreak over the divorce."

"Sorry to hear about that," Chris said. "I didn't even know you were married, or that you were practicing law for that matter. You have really grown out of sight."

Geraldine shrugged. "That's okay, when my parents moved to Florida it was expected that I would grow up and out of sight." She laughed. "I've always loved jurisprudence so I went to law school. As for my marriage, it lasted exactly six months."

"What?" Chris asked interestedly. "What happened?"

"Well, my husband," Geraldine said bitterly, "forgot to mention that he was not originally born male. That's the kind of deception I can't live with; we knew each other for years. Had to sue him/her/ it for fraud."

"That's unbelievable," Chris said astonished. "How could you not know? I mean was there a... you know...penis?"

Geraldine laughed. "You'd be amazed at how real genital reassignment looks and feels."

Chris cleared his throat uncomfortably. "I am sorry to hear

about it."

Geraldine settled back in her chair, "that's not the really bad part, I mean I could probably stay and see how best to deal with the whole sorry mess but that beast had the nerve to cheat on me with another man. I thought my husband was gay. Then he explained that he was not technically gay because he was born a girl."

She shook her head in disgust. "Enough about me." she drew out her notepad. "Let's talk about you."

Chris was still processing the gruesome scenario she had painted, he stammered a bit. "I had an...an...affair."

Geraldine nodded. "I heard."

"She had a child, which she denied was mine at first but he is obviously mine. He looks just like me and my Dad, he has the trademark Donahue eyes, nose... everything."

"We will still need a court ordered DNA." Geraldine scribbled the information down. "Looking like you is not scientific evidence."

Chris sighed and shrugged. "I am not sure I should pursue this, Geraldine."

Geraldine stopped scribbling and watched him silently.

He put his chin in his hand. "I felt so guilty over the whole affair. I had promised her husband—who is still with her and raising my child with her—that I would stay away from them. A year later I hired a PI and then next thing I know, I am involved again. I saw him in person the other day at a friends wedding and I wanted to just hold him. He doesn't know me. I am a stranger. That sucks."

"Mmmm." Geraldine nodded. "What you are feeling is not unusual. There are several cases where a parent has relinquished all rights to a child but then change their mind because of a change in circumstances or emotions. Some of them have even successfully fought in the courts to reinstate their rights.

"In your case you didn't formally sign a document to relinquish your rights. However, under the law, a child that is born within a marriage is considered to be the offspring of the married couple. Except, of course, if the husband formally indicates that the child is not his. Are you following me so far?"

Chris nodded.

"This is clearly not the case." Geraldine crossed her legs and leaned forward. "This child is wanted and loved by everybody. It will be an uphill battle for you to even get this case aired. As far as I know, the mother is Kelly Palmer."

Chris nodded again.

"Her father plays golf with most of the judges in this side of Jamaica, and he is rich."

Chris shrugged. "I do business with him. His supermarket is the official supplier of several of our hotels."

"Okay." Geraldine scratched her head. "Obviously you are both well off. It is going to be a toss up between who is more influential and who is craftier."

"What?" Chris frowned, "I don't like how this is going. Maybe I should leave well enough alone. As my brother-in-law keeps harping on, 'if it ain't broke'..."

"Hold it right there," Geraldine said, "I am good at crafty but we have to have a plan. No judge in his or her right mind would give a single man custody of a three year old. Especially if that three year old is in a happy stable environment, with two parents."

Chris sighed.

"That's if we can even get a court ordered DNA."

Chris sighed again and put his head in his hands.

"The parents may stall you forever if you ask for a DNA test," Geraldine said while tapping her pen on her cheek.

"And then again, they may tell you no outright. They would be very opposed to your butting into their lives. The husband is a pastor, is he not?" Geraldine asked contemplatively.

"Yes he is," Chris replied, "but you know that already. I am sure my mother had to tell you that."

"Oh she did, which makes this whole thing that much tougher. He is a moral figure in society, a good man who loves his wife. They have created a loving environment with their children. They are into charities and are helping people."

She sighed. "The only option I can foresee is for you to get married and be on a level playing field with them."

Chris snapped up his head and looked at Geraldine shocked. "Are you crazy?"

"Nope," Geraldine said seriously, "you will have to level the playing field. As it is, you are single. You have had an affair with a married woman and you may have a bitter girl or two from your past who would be willing to say that you are the worst man to have ever walked the earth. You need to appear stable and grounded to have a judge look at this case. Being married indicates that you aren't a young playboy who is maliciously seeking to destroy a family because of your own selfish desires to claim your son, just because he looks like you."

"It's not like that," Chris said aghast, "I genuinely love him, I can't explain it. I just do."

Geraldine shrugged. "Marriage is the only answer I can come up with and even then that it is still a long-shot. When you get married, we'll give it six months, and then we'll file for a court ordered DNA. Then we'll sue for custody. Six months is a long enough time to establish that you are serious about the marriage, I think. It is best to marry someone who understands the whole situation and is willing to get married to you on short notice."

She flipped through her calendar. "I am free tomorrow, if you want to start the year right. I wouldn't mind being married to a real man for a change."

Chris realized that his mouth was hung open when it snapped shut, a noise that actually made him jump.

Was Geraldine out of her mind? He didn't even know her and could vaguely recall seeing her as a little girl. And now here she was, her diary opened gazing at him in anticipation to get married so that he could file for a DNA test sometime in the future, which may or may not come through.

He didn't take marriage so lightly. Not even for his precious baby son would he even think of doing it.

"Geraldine...er..." Chris got up from his desk reluctantly. "Marriage is something I thought I would have done years ago with Kelly. Since then I have not even had the slightest urge to get married to anyone."

Except, he suddenly saw in his minds eye, Pinky with a stubborn look on her face saying, 'I am not coming back to work for you because I have feelings for you.'

Would she say yes if he proposed?

The thought gave him pause. Could he spend the rest of his life with Pinky? He could actually see himself with her. There wouldn't be a dull day in his life, that was for sure, and eventually he could grow to love her.

He rubbed his hands in anticipation. "Sorry Geraldine, I have someone else in mind."

Geraldine shrugged. "I can't say that I am particularly hurt, but that was fast. This person you have in mind, is she a responsible and upright citizen and over the age of eighteen years?"

Chris shrugged. "I had her in mind a long time ago, if I am to be honest with myself, this will just expedite things a bit.

Yes she's responsible, has not had any run-ins with the law. She's finishing up a chemistry degree."

Geraldine glanced at her watch. "Okay then, give me a call when you have reached the three month mark. I will contact the Palmer's and feel them out. Scare them a little, make them sweat for even thinking that they could keep your child away from you."

She kissed him on the cheek. " Happy new year when it comes."

Chris nodded. "Same to you too and thanks."

*****

He put on his jogging clothes when Geraldine left and went downstairs to the basement where he had a fully equipped gym. He really needed to run off some steam, clear his head and think about this whole marriage issue.

If he proposed to Pinky he couldn't tell her why he was doing it. If he got married and succeeded in sharing custody with Theo and Kelly, he could imagine that they would be far from pleased.

He maxed the treadmill and started running. Oh what a tangled web we weave when first we practice to deceive. The uninvited thought came into his head and he squelched it.

He couldn't pretend that he didn't want Pinky. He didn't love her but he really wanted her in his life and in his bed.

Wasn't it time he settled down anyhow? Everyone wanted him to. That's all his mother talked about these days and his family was usually holding their breath waiting for him to get involved with someone. Well they would have the opportunity. He was going to do it; he was going to propose to Pinky Black.

Chapter Ten

Pinky alighted from Lance's car on Wednesday evening, the day before the New Year. It was going to be one of those humdrum New Year's Eve nights; she could feel it already.

Charles was spending his time with Tanya. She was going to be stuck watching television, seeing everybody having fun and ringing in the New Year with jocularity and bonhomie, while she stuffed her face with her mother's leftover dinner, feeling sorry for herself.

She sighed when Lance drove off and was about to go into the yard when Chris drove up in his BMW SUV. He rolled down the window almost as soon as he stopped and stared at her with a small smile at his lips.

"I was timing you. It seems as if I got here on time."

Pinky stared back at him, her heart doing that little quiver that it always did when Chris was in her vicinity.

"I am not coming back to work for you," Pinky said, her

voice a mere whisper. "I am hardening my heart against you. I told you that this morning over the phone."

Chris ran his eyes over her, taking in her blue dress and her matching blue shoes; she looked simply elegant and so adorable with that defiant look in her brown gaze.

"My parents have this thing every year before the New Year starts. The entire family gathers together on my mother's back porch, we give God thanks for his numerous blessings, we hold hands and pray and then we eat, listen to music and chat."

Pinky frowned. "So?"

"You are dressed for it. Why don't you come with me?"

"Oh no," Pinky said, gripping her bag closer to her, "you are not dragging me into your family time. This is one of those mixed signals that you give me, one minute you are hot and next minute you are cold." She shuddered. "I don't want to catch a Donahue flu. Thanks but no thanks."

"Donahue flu?" Chris laughed. "Pinky, come on. My family wants to meet you."

Pinky spun around, her eyes wide with questions. "Are you asking me as a..." she cleared her throat. "Is this a date?"

Chris nodded. He got out of the car and leaned on it folding his arms. He was in a green shirt and a black pants. He looked tall muscular and delicious.

Pinky licked her lips. "Why?"

"Why what?" Chris asked her wearily.

"Why are you suddenly asking me on a date?"

"Because I like you," Chris said walking slowly towards her, "I want my family to know you."

Pinky closed her eyes when he stood in front of her; he was close enough that she could feel his body heat. "Stop playing with me, I have feelings."

"I know." Chris whispered, he lowered his face toward her

and kissed her slowly—the kiss went on for eons. He took his time exploring her soft pillow like pink lips. Pinky was so weak she clung to him helplessly.

When Chris raised his head he looked shaken. "Wow."

Pinky picked up her bag, which had fallen when he was kissing her, and brushed it off.

"Okay, let me put this down."

She barely glanced at him when she let herself into the house—her legs were shaking. So that was what it was like to really kiss Chris Donahue.

*****

Pinky didn't know what to expect when she went to meet Chris' family. The Donahues were so well respected and spoken of in such hushed tones of reverence that she was expecting a group of stiff upper lip people who air-kissed and said 'dahling.'

She was in for a big surprise. Chris' family was quite pleasant. He had five nieces and nephews, who ganged him as soon as he stepped through the imposing front door.

"Uncle Chris!"

"Uncle Chris!"

His sister Camille, who looked very much like a female version of Chris, was waiting eagerly to meet her at the door.

She hugged Pinky tightly and grinned. "It's lovely to meet you Pinky. Let me introduce you around, I'll start with my husband Kenneth."

Kenneth nodded at her politely. "Lovely to meet you." He looked like a body builder; he was huge with bulging biceps and shaved head. His brown eyes were warm though, and he had crinkles at the side of his eyes that made him look like he laughed a lot. He was pouring out drinks from what looked like a bar in a huge sitting room.

"And these are my sisters, Marie and Fiona." The two ladies were sitting; they jumped up when Pinky entered the room and hugged her just as enthusiastically as Camille had done.

Marie looked like she could be a model. She was extremely beautiful; had cat like hazel eyes, and a cheeky grin.

Fiona was assessing Pinky and when their eyes collided Fiona looked into her eyes unrepentantly as if she wanted to ferret out some secrets there.

Camille introduced her to their husbands and some more extended family. Their patio was huge with marble tiles in a honey color and a natural pool with slabs of stone in the middle of a waterfall. It looked tranquil and soothing.

Camille was heading for an older couple that were laughing and talking on the far deck. Pinky knew them to be Chris' parents. She had seldom seen Hyacinth Donahue close up but she recognized that elegant frame any day, and that way that she held herself, which shouted pure class.

The gentleman was a taller, older version of Chris. The genes in the family were strong, Pinky could see. The thought came to her that poor Kelly picked the wrong man to get pregnant for. Even the grandchildren, who had reluctantly left their uncle, had the same hazel-eyed curly hair look.

Chris walked rapidly to Pinky's side. "I'll introduce her properly to the parents." He said to Camille.

Camille smiled at them both and left.

When they reached the couple Hyacinth Donahue turned to them. Harlan had on a pleasant smile but Hyacinth was frowning.

"Mom, Dad, this is Petrina Black, otherwise called Pinky."

"Oh, hello Petrina," Harlan said gently. He took her hand and clasped it firmly. Hyacinth smiled at her but Pinky could see that it hadn't quite reached her eyes.

"Miss Black." she nodded in Pinky's direction.

Chris sighed, "Mom come on."

Hyacinth sniffed. "Excuse me. I have to check on the hors d'oeuvres. The extended family should be here any minute now."

She walked off elegantly with her head held high. Pinky looked at Chris askance. "What's the matter with her?"

"Hates your guts," Harlan said laughing, "but don't worry, she hates everybody who our Chris likes. There is nobody good enough for her little boy."

Chris grinned. "Perish the thought, I am thirty-three. Sorry Pinky, my Mom will come around. Somebody will tackle her in the kitchen and remind her that she's a Christian and then she'll come back out, and be on her best behavior."

Pinky nodded, a pleased smile on her face. So Chris had told his family that he liked her. Not even his mother's attitude could dampen her spirits.

She felt like flying. She didn't know what she had expected but it wasn't the realization that Chris Donahue actually liked her enough to have told his family about her. She looked at him with shining eyes. He looked back at her and squeezed her hands gently.

*****

One week later, Chris sorted through his mail on Thursday. As usual his hands clenched the Manila envelop from Cayman. He took out the pictures of Mark, setting aside the ones with him and Kelly or Theo and just focusing on his cute little face he sat down into a chair. Mark was in a green cap and was grinning. He had in all his teeth now and was happily showing off all his pearly whites for the camera.

Chris traced the picture lovingly and put it down with a sigh. His quest to win Pinky over was working like a charm. He carried her out and listened while she prattled on and on about whatever subject interested her.

He was thinking of proposing to her tonight. He could be married by the second week in January, that way his sisters could be here when he tied the knot and he could be well on his way with this custody case for Mark.

He pictured Kelly and Theo's face when his lawyer called and smiled to himself. They had no idea what was coming to them.

"Knock—knock," Camille said floating into his office smiling, "it is so good to see you smile again."

Chris' smile grew wider. "I have decided that I am going to propose to Pinky tonight."

Camille frowned. "Chris, please don't use that girl in this custody case. She's lovely… she genuinely loves you. I can't help but think that this is wrong."

Chris leaned back in his chair. "I like her and she loves me. She wants to marry me."

"Marriage is serious business Chris." Camille sat down across from him. "I wonder if that affair with Kelly has skewed your concept of what a serious commitment marriage is."

Chris shrugged. "My concept of marriage is fine."

"No, it's not," Camille said knowingly, "or you would not have had that affair with Kelly."

She flung her hair over her shoulders. "Don't marry her," Camille said with a warning in her voice, "you need help to sort out your feelings and to get this whole thing into perspective. Maybe I've been wrong in pushing you to get access to Mark. Maybe you should go to counseling with a Christian counselor, somebody who will also pray with you about this."

"If I marry her it will be the first step toward getting Mark," Chris said with a stubborn look to his chin. "It's not as if I don't like her. I do. I like everything about her. Well most things." He scratched his chin.

"This is not going to end well," Camille warned him. "Marrying to get custody of your child, not a good idea. Why on earth are you listening to Geraldine anyway? How long has she been practicing law?"

Chris shrugged. "I don't know but she made a very good point, I have no rights where my own flesh and blood is concerned because he was born in wedlock to a man who wants him. Getting married myself might be the only avenue I have available to me. When I am in a family environment myself, then I'll make a move."

"But will Pinky agree with that move?" Camille asked with concern. "As far as I can see from Pinky she is not a doormat kind of girl."

"We'll cross that bridge when we get to it," Chris said stubbornly.

Camille flung one leg over the arm of her chair and stared at her brother wearily. "I had no idea you were so ruthless."

*****

Chris headed to Pinky's place in Flatbush with that thought ringing in his head. Was he ruthless? Or was he just a concerned father who wanted to see more of his child? Pinky loved him; she said it over and over again. He would break her heart if he married anybody but her.

Surely he wasn't using her. He'd be a good husband. The best husband he could be. He would try his utmost best to be there for her when she needed him, and give her the support and the attention that all women craved. He would not give her any cause to look outside their marriage.

The idea horrified him when he gave it thought. Having deceived Theo with Kelly he had this fear that should he get married there would be some retribution through his own marriage, adultery wise.

He had no idea how he would treat infidelity in his marriage, the very thought made him sick. He sighed when he drove up to her gate. He grimaced at the irony of his thoughts. It was amazing how the human mind could justify wrongdoing but balk at the very same thing when on the receiving end.

There was a large moving truck beside the house that he heard that Phoebe used to live in. Charles was sitting on the gate bare-chested and looking on the proceedings.

"What's going on?" Chris asked him.

"Phoebe is moving out her parent's stuff. Apparently, she is going to renovate the house or something. She moved them to a small estate where her father can farm and her mother can play the lady of the manor."

Chris whistled. "That's good of her. I always got the feeling that her mother was the one who made her into a little monster."

Charles grinned. "She told me how she used to stalk you."

Chris shivered. "With a determination that many private investigators would only dream of."

"Tanya said she's honeymooning in the Seychelles, apparently her husband has a whole island there."

Chris nodded absently. In all of his planning to ask Pinky to marry him the thought of a honeymoon hadn't really been at the forefront of his mind. A week or two of just getting to know her body sounded like a splendid idea. Finally, he would be making love to somebody who was his, who wouldn't leave him because she loved somebody else.

"Where's Pinky?" Chris asked with anticipation lacing his tones.

"In the house titivating for you." Charles looked at him hardly. "Don't hurt my sister. I don't understand why you are suddenly paying her so much attention and I don't trust it."

Chris paused. "Well your intuition is wrong, I am not going to hurt her, I am going to ask her to marry me tonight."

Charles inhaled sharply. "Why? I mean a few weeks ago you fired her from her job and now you want to marry her?"

"I need her." Chris said honestly. "I function much better when she's around."

He spun around when he heard footsteps on the veranda and there was Pinky in a bright orange dress, which hit her just above her knee and hugged her in the right places. Chris moaned, a low growl that came from the depths of his throat. Every time he saw her, his body tingled in all the right places.

Charles laughed beside him. "Yes, she's all that. Good genes."

Chris barely glanced at him as Pinky came down the steps, her pink lips glistening with lip-gloss.

He felt like asking her 'will you marry me now' this minute, and then drag her off to the nearest pastor where they could get the deed done and then hauling her off to his bed.

Instead, he cleared his throat. "You look beautiful as usual."

Pinky laughed. "Thank you, former boss man."

She air kissed Charles and headed to the vehicle.

Chris opened the door for her and couldn't help but look at her legs for a long time. When he looked up Pinky was blushing.

"You really know how to turn on the sexy," she purred.

She gazed into his limpid hazel eyes and then moved forward to kiss him. It was one of those deep soul searching kisses that had both of them panting like dogs in heat.

They tore apart when they heard cheers. The moving men and Charles were whooping and clapping.

Chris put his forehead on hers, "Pinky, you love me right?"

Pinky's eyes were at half-mast, "yes I do."

"Wouldn't it be nice if we did this the right way, get married instead of burning with all of this sexual heat?"

Pinky gasped. "Is that a proposal?"

Chris pulled away from her and then kissed her softly. "I guess."

"Then ask me properly." Pinky said excitedly.

Chris groaned and went around to the driver's side, "I have never felt so sexually aroused in my life." He leaned back in his seat. "Maybe you should change into something else. Something less sexy if we are going to spend the rest of the evening together."

"Are you serious?" Pinky asked.

"Yes I am," Chris looked at her hotly, "that's why I never wanted to take this anywhere when you worked for me. I know my limitations, and you are one sexy woman. I was determined not go down the route of casual sex again. So yes Pinky, I am serious."

Pinky scrambled out of the car. "I do have a long dress that's a bit slack in the sides."

"And cover your head too, wear a hat and take off that lip gloss," Chris said wiping his lips; he had on some of her lip-gloss from the kiss.

"You are crazy," Pinky said lovingly. "I am only changing my dress."

She headed into the house. Charles was watching the two of them with a puzzled expression on his face. When she came back out in a long black dress, he busted out laughing.

"Shut up," Pinky said snarling. She got into the car smiling at Chris. "So am I decent now?"

"No," Chris groaned. "Your lips are bare and juicy. I was going to drive us to a restaurant maybe the caves, after much romantic music and good food, I'd pop the question."

"Oh Chris," Pinky's eyes were wet, "I never dreamed that this would happen. I always thought that you'd be so locked up in your emotions with Kelly and all of that angst over your son that you wouldn't love me for me."

Chris stiffened slightly. "Pinky I never said love but I do need you. I need you so much I can taste it. Will you marry me?"

Pinky didn't hesitate. Later when she was in bed and going over his proposal word for word she would pause, but not now.

"Yes!" she squealed in his ear and hugged him so tight that he was gasping for air.

"Would you mind if we got married next week?" Chris asked looking into her big brown eyes.

"No," Pinky said kissing him all over the face, "next week today. Any time is fine by me."

*****

It was a small ceremony held on the seaside at Villa Rose in the morning. Daryl Brick, the presiding pastor from three rivers Church was not that pleased to perform the ceremony, but it wasn't evident from the wide smile that he wore that last night he had argued with the groom long into the night about getting married without counseling. He didn't agree with Chris rushing to the altar.

The parents looked a little shell-shocked. The Donahues were not as stunned as the Blacks but the general feeling in the air was one of incredulity on both sides.

The bride couldn't care less, she had been proposed to

exactly seven days before and she had gotten her dress the very next day. An off the shoulder white dress which emphasized her toned arms and cinched in her flat waist. She had taken out her blonde braids on the third day leading up to the wedding and had dyed her hair a modest chestnut hair color with reddish highlights. She looked adorable and sexy and the groom was very pleased with his choice; so much so that he had at times forgotten why he was going through with the ceremony. The lines were being blurred in his head and he forgot everyone and everything else but Pinky while he was staring in her eyes during the ceremony.

"I now pronounce you husband and wife," Pastor Brick said. There were a few restrained claps heard in the small gathering and a few surprised faces among the group.

"You may kiss your bride," Pastor Brick added a note of jocularity in his voice.

Chris kissed Pinky a brief kiss with a promise of more to come.

She had a smile a mile wide and was laughing when they turned to face her family and a few of her friends who were around before the school semester started.

"Let me get this straight," Hyacinth Donahue said while walking up to Chris, who was sipping orange juice and talking to Camille. Pinky was with her family who still had a dazed expression in their eyes. "You married this girl to get custody of Mark?"

Chris nodded.

"You were avoiding me all week, weren't you?" Hyacinth asked fiercely, "I couldn't get to you all week, until this fiasco. Chris what is the matter with you? First you have an affair, now you get married to get access to the child of that affair. What happens when that poor girl is dumped by you because you still love Kelly?"

Chris had a grin on his lips but it slowly died while his mother was talking. "Mom it's not like that, not even close. I like her and marriages have been built on less."

Hyacinth shook her head furiously. "What did I ever do in raising you that caused you to be like this?"

Camille was standing as silent as a statue. Marie and Fiona had walked up to them as Hyacinth tore into him furiously.

She exhaled roughly. "I wasn't going to come to this shenanigan but your father who must be going soft in his head said he had a feeling this would all work out."

She gripped Chris' hand, tears in her eyes. "I am sorry."

"Sorry for what Mom?" Chris asked his agitated mother.

"Sorry for introducing you to Geraldine. She was a bit unconventional in her approach, but the truth is, I had a small hope that the two of you would get together. Why on earth did she encourage you to go this far?"

"Because she doesn't respect marriages," Fiona said scornfully. "I blame all of this on you Mom."

"Hold up," Chris said fiercely to his sisters. "This marriage isn't even a couple minutes old and you all are standing around and mourning its demise. In case you haven't noticed this is supposed to be a happy affair."

"Affair," Camille said scornfully. She was in a burgundy dress with a pearl encrusted bodice. "That word affair. I loathe it. It is the reason for this."

"This marriage will work," Chris said stubbornly, "the deed is done. Pinky is a lovely girl."

"What kind of name is Pinky?" Hyacinth said huffing. "Here comes the blushing bride," she said as Pinky advanced toward them. "I'm not going to act like I'm happy about this," Hyacinth said. "Excuse me." She walked off dabbing her eyes.

Chris' sisters all stared at him with varying levels of

reproach and suddenly he felt as if he had done a very bad thing. Why were his choices in life so bad that he had mini crises one after the other?

Pinky walked up to her brand new husband and his sisters a radiant beam in her eye. "I love you Christopher Donahue."

Chris kissed her on her forehead and gave his sisters the evil eye. "Ladies excuse me."

They murmured something and walked away.

"What's the matter with everybody here?" Pinky asked impatiently. "They are acting as if this is a funeral and not a wedding. My mother was just crying and my father is only grunting."

Chris looked into her eyes deeply. "This is going to work Pinky."

"Of course it will, silly." Pinky hit him playfully. "I am going to be the best and only wife you'll ever have."

"I requested that my brother who is acting in the capacity of deejay play this song for us." She looked into his eyes lovingly, when the song 'By Your Side' by Sade began playing.

"Love this song and the sentiments are from me to you."

They danced slowly to the song and Chris wondered uncomfortably if she would mean them in a few months time.

Chapter Eleven

Chris may not be so sure about his marriage but he was sure about his wedding night and all the nights that were to come. They had barely got through the door of their honeymoon suite at Villa Rose when he started to undress his pocket-sized wife. She was eagerly helping him out of his clothes too.

"Aren't you going to change into some night gown or the other?" He asked her panting as he undid the buttons at the back of her dress.

"No," Pinky said a languid look in her eyes, "I am Petrina Donahue and I have waited all year for this." She giggled uncontrollably as he replaced his hand with his mouth.

He took pleasure in exploring her dips and plains and arousing her to fever pitch.

They spent hours in their suite without food just loving each other. When they finally relented in the middle of the night, Chris called down to the kitchen for room service.

"Oh no," Pinky groaned jokingly, "they are going to know that I haven't eaten all day, and that I've been up here doing unspeakable things to the boss."

Chris his hair ruffled and a satisfied look in his eyes kissed her. "Now you are Mrs. Boss. Stop acting bashful."

They heard a knock on the door.

"Room service."

Pinky hurriedly put on her diaphanous robe and padded into the bathroom.

Chris opened the door and saw that it was Caleb.

"Caleb Wright, you do not do room service," he said grinning. "What are you doing here?"

Caleb grinned, "I only caught the end of the wedding, sorry about that. It was so sudden and I had a previous appointment at the doctor's office with Kalice."

"Is she okay?" Chris asked concerned, the baby was almost three months old.

"She's fine." Caleb said, looking around curiously. "I left her there with Erica who came by late. It's a long boring domestic story. Where's your new wife?"

"Hiding out in the bathroom."

Caleb laughed and wheeled the tray and started setting up the table things. "Why the sudden rush to get married?" he lowered his voice.

Chris could barely hear him, he was whispering so low. "Is it because Kelly is pregnant again and you just want to prove that you have moved on?"

"What? I didn't know about that?" Chris asked a sudden rush of blood going to his head.

A shaft of jealousy hit him from out of nowhere. She is pregnant again?

She didn't look pregnant in the last set of Thursday pictures he got. So now his son would be probably neglected to make way for their new reconciliation baby.

"Baby number four is on the way," Caleb whispered, he finished setting out the table and looked at Chris seriously, "I am so happy you have moved on from Kelly. Pinky is a great girl."

He gave Chris' frozen expression an assessing look before wheeling out of the room and then shook his head in resignation before closing the door.

Chris felt a mixture of emotions when he sat down at the table. He felt jealousy and a curious pain. Why couldn't he just cut off the emotions where Kelly was concerned? Thinking of her was like poking a partially healed sore with a knife. He glanced across at a grinning Pinky, who had sauntered out of the bathroom in a very sexy negligee and had sat down at the table an impish smile on her face.

She was eating ice cream and licking the spoon suggestively, her antics registered on his anatomy but his emotions were going haywire.

Kelly was pregnant.

He could recall very vividly the last time he heard that; he had gone through feverish agonies wondering if the child was his. When she started avoiding him all together he had gone as far as to get her doctor to tell him her due date. It hadn't been easy but he had found out that the doctor patient confidentiality had a price too.

He had ping-ponged between ecstasy and a pending sense of doom. The thoughts had almost crippled him until he had found out conclusively that she had had his baby. The relief had been intense. He had wanted them to start up their own family. Looking back now he had been quite naive.

Why did this latest pregnancy of hers fill him with such despair? Was he a sucker for punishment?

There was a perfectly good woman sitting across from him. He had been her first lover and she was extremely willing to try everything with him and was ecstatically happy with him. But here he was brooding about a past love.

He tried to temper the thoughts to the back of his mind and the old partially healed sores that had Kelly's name on them.

Caleb was calculating with his information—Caleb had deliberately told him about Kelly's pregnancy to test him. Chris had had failed the test. He had stood in the middle of the room like he was made from stone; listening to the figurative stitches on his old wounds pinging off one-by-one.

He stared at Pinky not really seeing her. But Pinky, thinking that he was responding to her had a triumphant look in her eyes. Chris smiled at her wickedly. Sure that the smile hadn't reached his eyes—maybe she could help him forget. He crooked his finger at her.

*****

Pinky adjusted her sunglasses on her nose and tried to get lost in the scenery. She was lounging at the beach with Chris four weeks after their hasty marriage and her mind had just started to process the fact that she was Mrs. Chris Donahue.

It was a whirlwind month. She moved back into Chris' house with a grinning Maud calling her Mrs. Donahue and welcoming her home.

Living with Chris felt a little different, she slept in his room now and he did take pains to include her in conversations but Pinky, couldn't fight the nagging feeling that there was a huge chunk of Chris that was buried and kept out of her reach.

She had been so on top of the world being married to him that she hadn't really paused to assess why Chris had married her. She hadn't cared that it was rather sudden and that he did seem to be overwhelmed with passion for her.

Each time she asked a question that was remotely important he distracted her with sex. She wasn't complaining, but there was a part of him that was closed off and brooding and she had a sneaky foreboding that it had something to do with Kelly.

He was always this way when it had anything to do with that woman and her child, Pinky thought resentfully. She had wanted to ask him if he still got his weekly correspondence from Cayman but a little part of her was reluctant to hear the answer. She preferred to live in utopia in her head. After all, she was living her fantasy. The man she loved married her in a whirlwind ceremony and they were now living happily ever after. This was the after, and she loved it. She stretched sinuously and glanced at him.

His busybody mother seemed to be everywhere. When she worked for Chris, she couldn't remember a time when he had to go to Sunday Brunch at his parents place every Sunday. Now all of a sudden, Chris' presence was mandatory and she had to tag along to these ridiculous gatherings, so she had countered the Sunday Brunch with Sunday Beach.

She loved going to the beach and it was something that she wanted Chris to share with her. Besides, she had wanted some excuse not to attend his parents' brunch. His mother treated her with a vague dislike that always had Pinky feeling inadequate.

Chris had reminded her that they had brunch at eleven. She glanced at her watch it was just nine o' clock—she wasn't looking forward to it.

Hyacinth Donahue was wound tighter than a string. She looked as if she wanted to tell off Pinky for something or the other. Pinky wondered briefly what was so objectionable about her person that made Mrs. Donahue dislike her so much.

Was it something she said or did? Was it the fact that she wasn't from a wealthy background?

She discounted that quickly. Chris' family wasn't snobbish in the least, and Harlan seemed to genuinely like her. So what was Hyacinth's problem?

And what was Chris' problem? He was staring off into space and clenching his teeth in agony. She found herself asking him, involuntarily, what was wrong; he was really acting as if he was in pain.

"Nothing's wrong," Chris said smiling at her. He turned his body to hers in the lounge chair and kissed her on the tip of her ear.

"You have your sun glasses on, I can't see your eyes." Pinky pushed her glasses onto her forehead and looked into her reflection in his. "Take them off."

"No," Chris said turning away from her, "not a chance."

Pinky frowned. "You are hiding something aren't you?"

"Whatever could I be hiding?" Chris asked translucently. "Everything is fine."

"No, it's not," Pinky said sitting up straighter in the lounge chair, "I'm not completely naive you know. I can tell when you are hurting over something."

She glanced at him uncertainly and then she started fiddling with the tassels at the bottom of her jeans shorts. "Do you love me Chris?"

Chris sat up straighter too, his cheeks flinching a bit from the question. He took her hands into his and slowly caressed her fingers. "I can't answer that right now."

"You can't because you don't." Pinky got up and stretched. "You don't love me, I can tell. You are obsessing over Kelly aren't you?"

Chris shrugged. He pushed the glasses up onto his forehead and looked at her. His bare chest had a few sprinklings of chest hair and he looked muscular and well defined. She found herself wishing contrarily that he wasn't so good-looking. His clear hazel eyes were staring at her with a mixture of regret and sadness.

"I thought you were over all of that," Pinky whispered. "I thought this whole marriage thing was a declaration that you were willing to start a new life, not just so we can have legal sex!"

She glared at Chris fulsomely. "Please take me home, I'm not going to your mother's little brunch thing today. I need to think."

"Pinky, it's not like..."

She put her fingers on his lips, "I am not going to be the person who will force you to tell me lies so that I can feel better. I just need to adjust my rose spectacles a bit—dim it somewhat, okay?"

Chris nodded, kissing her fingers. She withdrew them tremblingly and gave a deep sigh.

*****

Two weeks later, on Thursday, Chris brought in the mail. He slowly opened the envelope and scanned through the pictures. His eager eyes searched Kelly's body for any hint of a pregnancy.

In one of them, she was holding Mark. She was dressed in a tight pink dress and laughing. She didn't look pregnant to him but she looked disgustingly happy. He flung the pictures in the bin and briefly wondered where Pinky was at the moment. He had left her at house early that morning. She had been frantically trying to find some lab paraphernalia she had misplaced.

He vaguely recalled her saying that she was going to the beach after her lab with Charles and his friends. They really loved the beach Chris thought and then he snatched up his car keys and got up impatiently.

He could either stay here and be stuck with his thoughts or he could go to the beach with his wife and see what was so fascinating to her and her friends about the beach.

He had generously offered for them to come up to the house and use the pool but so far Pinky kept her friends far from him. She had told him with a grin that he was too serious for her crowd. He had frowned at that statement.

She had kissed him on the cheek and said, "see what I mean?"

Chris put a determined smile on his face—though he knew it resembled more of a grimace—and pulled up close to the spot where he saw the bus that they usually piled in to go to the beach.

Pinky had driven her car; he had given her a late model Honda that she was having fun driving around. He had seen the bright red color and knew that it was the right type of vehicle for her.

He got out of the car and pocketed the keys. He had no real intention of swimming today; he just wanted to escape his thoughts.

He searched for them on the beach, which was nearly empty. Then he heard singing and laughing and squealing under a palm tree. From a distance his eyes could make out Pinky who was in a bright pink bikini running along the shore and being captured by one of her friends. The guy grabbed her in a football tackle and was tickling her and making growling noises. She was doubled up in paroxysms of laughter, the other young people were laughing at both of their antics.

The jealousy came gradually. It wasn't sharp like a knife cut, it was more like a sea wave slowly rolling into shore then crashing onto the sea side, he actually looked out at the sea, taking his eyes away from Pinky being mauled by another man. He felt like acting irrational, and commanding her to stop having fun with her male friend and stop being so familiar with these young people.

Something alerted Pinky that she was being watched and when she raised her head she saw Chris in the distance. He had his hands stuck into his pockets, an unyielding stiff look to his profile.

That was his defensive look, Pinky thought troubled. What was he doing at the beach anyway? She had invited him several times but he had refused to come along with her and her friends.

"Howie stop tickling me." Pinky hauled herself up from the sand. "I think I see my husband over there. Going to see if something is wrong."

"Ah, isn't that sweet?" Howie said laughing. "He can't bear for you to be away from him for long."

Pinky furrowed her brows in consternation. In her fantasy world that may have been true, but in real life she knew that Chris didn't love her and that he could bear to be away from her. So far, she hadn't really cared. Not everybody will be loved like they should be, she reasoned. She had appreciation, which was good, most of her friends went on an on about not being appreciated and Chris liked and needed her. That should be enough for now.

She walked slowly over to Chris.

He turned to face her, a stormy look in his eyes. "Why was that guy touching you like that?"

"Hello to you too grumps," Pinky said looking at Chris

with surprise in her eyes. "How was your day?"

Chris hunched his shoulders. The wind had picked up and was whipping its way across the sea.

"You are dressed indecently—having men touching you all over your body. So this is what you guys do at the beach?"

"This is how people in the twenty-first-century dress at the beach Sourpuss," Pinky said putting her hands akimbo. "And Howie is my friend from high school, whose girlfriend is sitting right over there beside Charles."

"I don't like this whole set up," Chris said frowning.

"Because you are paranoid," Pinky said laughing. "Want to join us? My friends are a little afraid of you. This would be a good time to show them you are human."

"I am having a crisis of jealousy here," Chris said seriously, "why are you treating this so lightly?"

"Because you have nothing to be jealous about," Pinky said exasperatedly. "You have gone from brooding and dark to jealous and suspicious."

She hugged him snuggling her face into his chest. "I like it."

"You like it?" Chris looked down at her sandy tipped hair incredulously.

"Yes," Pinky sighed, "shows you have a thing for me."

She looked up into his face with an impish grin on her face. "You were jealous of Howie. I must never tell him that, he'd be happy for weeks."

"Let's go home," Chris kissed her on the forehead.

"Sure thing," Pinky said releasing him. "I'm gonna get my things."

Chapter Twelve

Mid-April

Chris was pacing around his study with a cell phone in hand. He was married for three months to the day. Geraldine had said three months would be sufficient time for him to get the whole custody ball rolling.

He drummed his fingers on his desk impatiently and realized that he was still of two minds about calling Geraldine—his married life so far was really good. He hadn't laughed so much in years or had so much fun with a woman as he did with Pinky.

But the nagging feeling that his son would be third in Theo's menagerie just irked him a little bit too much. He would no longer be the baby or special. They'd probably have him wiping off the roof when it rained or treating him like the male version of Cinderella.

He tried to contain his paranoia but it kept building and building until finally he convinced himself that Mark needed to be saved from the Palmers.

He dialed Geraldine's number slowly and it rang twice. She came on the phone in her usual businesslike manner.

"Geraldine, it's Chris."

"Ah Chris," Geraldine said with a smile in her voice, "I heard that you got married, congratulations on your nuptials."

"Thanks." Chris said warmly.

"How is it going so far?"

"Very good actually." Chris bounced a stress ball on his desk that Pinky had given him several months ago, as a tongue-in-cheek present. "This is the three month mark, I am calling to set this whole custody thing in motion."

Geraldine cleared her throat. "Well, I will get to it right away and actually visit them today. I am in Cayman for the next four weeks. I have a corporate case dealing with. I will call first though, so I can speak with both of them."

"Kelly's pregnant." Chris said feeling the old irritation rise up again that had persisted when he first heard the news.

"Oh," Geraldine was silent for a while and sounded distracted, "all the better to strike when they are not fully aware of what is going on."

Chris felt a little tingle of regret at that but then he remembered that he was the injured party in all of this and said, "let me know how it goes."

"Sure thing Chris." Geraldine hung up the phone and swung around in her office chair. Well it wasn't really her office, it was borrowed space for the next two weeks, and then she'd be mainly working out of her hotel room.

She liked working in the Caribbean. The pace was way slower and though the various government systems were frustrating at times, she was enjoying the lack of frenetic activity.

She opened her address book and looked for the address for Theo Palmer; he lived on the East side. She would just hop on over after work and pay them a visit. Just to make sure that they would be around, she called first.

"Hello, good morning," a cultured voice came on the line.

"May I speak to Kelly Palmer please," Geraldine asked politely.

"This is she," Kelly answered, a note of weariness slipping into her voice.

"My name is Geraldine Brown, and I am the counsel for Christopher Donahue, representing him on a custody issue. I would like to meet with you and your husband later today, around six. Is that alright?"

"What custody issue?" Kelly asked outright panic taking over her voice.

"The custody of one Mark Donahue," Geraldine deliberately said in the sternest voice she could muster.

"I do not know of any Mark Donahue," Kelly said gasping.

"Oh sorry, a slip of the tongue," Geraldine said apologetically. "I believe you gave him your husband's name—Mark Palmer"

Kelly was silent.

"Is six o' clock alright Mrs. Palmer?" Geraldine asked stoutly. "If not, I could always leave it for another time. I am in Cayman for a couple of weeks."

"Six o' clock is fine," Kelly said after a long pause and hung up the phone with a click.

*****

Kelly stood in her sunny kitchen with a raging headache behind her eyes. When she got up this morning she had a strange foreboding that the day was not going to go well. She had gone through the motions: sent her children to school, kissed her husband goodbye before he left for work, carried her youngest to pre-school and had just stepped into the kitchen when the phone rang.

It was the call she had nightmares about. She had seen how Chris had looked at Mark at Phoebe's wedding and had begun having nightmares about him coming to snatch her son.

Her hands were trembling and she sat abruptly on a chair by the kitchen window. Why was he doing this now?

She had heard from an excited Erica, just three short months ago, that he had gotten married. At the time she had felt a mixture of joy and a curious feeling of jealousy, but she had quickly gotten over that. Chris had no place in her life now—her marriage was going from strength to strength and there was a new baby on the way. She was getting some really good jobs, professionally, and their home church felt like an extended family.

But now Chris decided to strike? When everything was going so well? She picked up the phone angrily and dialed Theo's number.

"Theo," her voice trembled a bit when he answered, "Chris' lawyer is coming to visit us at six o' clock this evening re a custody case."

Theo was silent for a long time then he cleared his throat. "Do you want me to come home now?"

"No." Kelly squeezed the phone. "It's just that…suppose he does get custody of Mark, or shared custody?" She started to sob. "I am so sorry, Theo."

"Oh hush, honey," Theo said comfortingly. He looked in his appointment book; he didn't have anything for the rest of the day that he couldn't be rescheduled. "I am coming home now. Don't stress out yourself you are four months pregnant."

Kelly whimpered and he got even more anxious. He hastily

hung up and spoke briefly to his secretary who was nodding understandably when he said he had a family emergency.

When he pulled up at the house and strolled into the kitchen, Kelly was hunched over the table sobbing.

Theo pulled her to himself and soothed her, almost frog marching her to the living room.

"Kelly, stop this," he said to her gently.

"But he's going to take away my baby." Kelly hiccupped.

"This is pregnancy hormones talking." Theo said rubbing her back. "Chris doesn't have a case. Remember I spoke to my lawyer friend Jeffrey and he said that Chris cannot legally claim Mark."

Kelly nodded and then hiccupped. "I am sorry I broke down. I just never expected this from Chris...at least not now...he's married for God's sake! Why would he want to trouble us now?"

Theo sighed. "Maybe he got married so that he could start the custody proceedings."

Kelly looked up at him, her big brown eyes wide with shock. "He wouldn't do that...would he?"

"It's possible," Theo said, "it's not unheard of. This shows that Chris is serious. And who can blame him? Mark looks exactly like him, he is growing up apart from him, and it must hurt."

"Whose side are you on?" Kelly asked suspiciously. "I'm not giving up my child."

"Nobody's asking you to." Theo wiped a stray tear from her cheek. "Let us just reason this out rationally, like adults. I have been thinking about this since Phoebe's wedding. I did ask him to leave us alone. I have since thought about how utterly unfair it was to deny Mark his heritage. He is a toddler now; he is no longer a babe in arms. He can do without you for weeks at a time."

"No," Kelly got up and held her pounding head, "why are you arguing like this?"

Theo sighed. "Kelly, listen to me for a minute, just sit down. I can see the veins bulging at the side of your head—calm down."

"I was happy," Kelly said frantically, "I was fine until this monster chose to come back into my life."

Theo looked at her quizzically. "Which monster?"

"Chris." Kelly huffed pacing up and down.

"Chris is not a monster," Theo said calmly, "your guilt is the monster."

"Stop using your counselor voice on me," Kelly said sitting across from him inelegantly, "I hate Chris."

Theo steepled his fingers under his chin. "I would prefer if you don't hate him."

Kelly rolled her eyes. "Why?"

"I don't hate him," Theo said relaxing back in his chair. "You are transferring the guilt and hate you feel about having an affair and projecting it all onto Chris. You need to stop it Kelly. Don't hate Chris on my account. I had forgiven you for that affair a long time ago. Every now and then I can see that you have not totally forgiven yourself. I am at a loss as to how to help you."

"I can't totally let it go," Kelly said her voice soft, "I constantly think about explaining why Mark does not look like Thea and Matthew and probably this new baby. I meet people in the supermarket who comment on how dissimilar he is to us. I am going to have to explain to people for the rest of my life why my son looks like a Donahue, and I hate that. I live with that everyday. Thea asked me the other night why Mark's eyes are green and nobody else's eyes in the family looks like his. I had to distract her. I am constantly trying not to lie to people and yet I see the speculation in their eyes."

"Then don't lie," Theo said to her earnestly. "We'll tell the children together that Mark has a different biological father. Maybe we'll do it before Chris' lawyer gets here tonight."

"They are not yet old enough to hear that," Kelly said fretfully. "They'll hate me when they find out."

"Ah, they'll never be old enough to hear," Theo said gently, "but it has to be done. We have always been honest with them and yet both of us have skirted around this issue—we have done so long enough. The affair did happen; you had a child as a result of it. Burying our heads in the sand hasn't done us any good.

We have never really dealt with the problem; we've brush it aside and we've pretended, but we've never dealt with it. Thea is twelve, a very bright twelve and Matt is ten. They will understand and they'll ask questions.

You don't have to go into details about the affair, but you do owe your children an explanation. These are the kinds of secrets that create so many family problems. If we are open about it now, it will spare you a load of heartache in the future."

"It's easy for you to say," Kelly said, feeling deflated. "You aren't the scarlet woman who has to confess her sins to her own children."

"Well I'll be here to support you Scarlet Woman and I really do think that Chris should be given some kind of access to Mark."

"No," Kelly said forcefully, "I don't want Chris back in my life."

Theo got up and loosened his tie; he held out his hand, "come here."

Kelly got up shakily.

He walked her to the bedroom and she stretched out on the

bed.

"Now listen to me carefully," Theo said soothingly. He sat at the foot of the bed and started massaging her feet. "I have felt guilty about keeping Mark away from Chris."

Kelly closed her eyes in pain. "It's my fault we are having this conversation."

Theo smiled. "Yes it is, but it happened, and now we have to deal with it. You don't have to be involved in Chris' life or he in ours..."

"But you just said..."

"I know what I said," Theo massaged her feet slowly. "Have you ever stopped to think about the fact that Mark will unavoidably meet up with his biological grandparents and cousins and even siblings when Chris has children of his own?"

"No." Kelly mumbled.

"The Donahues live a stones throw away from your parents, Kelly. We can't have Thea and Matthew spending time with your family and hide Mark. Caleb works with Chris at Villa Rose. They are friends. They all go to the same church...it's a small world.

"We may have moved to Cayman but we had still managed to run into Chris in less than three years. The children need to go to Jamaica for summer holidays this year, to spend time with their grandparents. There is no excuse why Mark shouldn't go."

"He is too young to travel." Kelly said hopefully.

Theo shook his head. "That may work this year, it may not work next year. And I don't think we should treat Mark any differently from the other children by holding him back from the rest of his family. We actually left him with a nanny to attend Erica's wedding. It's time we stopped hiding him. He is not a dirty secret. We don't want him to grow up thinking that he is different in a bad way."

"I hate this." Kelly closed her eyes. "Wake me up when everything is sorted out and I don't have to feel so ashamed."

Theo kissed her on the forehead. "We'll talk to the lawyer this evening and see what she has to say. Afterwards we'll deal with this together, you hear me?"

"I don't deserve you," Kelly said weakly. "I sometimes wake up in the nights and I hug you tight to me and wonder why I had to cheat, why I had to be dishonest." Her voice petered off.

Theo lay beside her and hugged her from behind. "That was the biggest test of our marriage, we got past it. God has been good to us. Now relax, I want Luke to be born without much trouble to you."

"Luke," Kelly giggled, "I should have known this child would be one of the gospels. Suppose it's a girl? "

"Then we'll name her Lucia—" Theo kissed her in her hair and listened to her gentle snoring, she'd be out like a light for most of the day. He carefully withdrew his arms from around her and then walked softly out of the room.

*****

When Geraldine arrived at the Spanish style home on East Side, the reception she got was not quite what she had expected. She was expecting hostility and strain. Instead, a handsome man with warm brown eyes opened the door.

He politely asked her to come in. She had stood there staring at him aghast. This was the husband and Kelly had cheated on him?

She had quickly regained her composure and walked in behind him into a comfortable living room.

"Please have a seat. My name is Theo Palmer," he said to

her.

"Er...my name is Geraldine...Geraldine Brown," she said briskly, struggling to sound as business like as she could. "Where is your wife? I'd like to talk to the both of you."

"She's in the kitchen overseeing supper," Theo replied politely.

He sat across from her. "You are Miss Angie Brown's granddaughter, the one who was doing law at Harvard, or was it Yale?"

"Yale," Geraldine said. "I almost forgot that you were the pastor at Three Rivers Church."

Theo nodded. "Lovely church. Miss Angie would give me a blow-by-blow account of what all her grandchildren were up to. I admired her determination to learn how to use the Internet in order to keep up with all of you."

Geraldine nodded. "I live with her now, I recently moved to Jamaica."

Theo nodded and then looked up. "Ah; here she is."

Kelly came into the room and sighed. "They are using the carrots as battleships."

She went over to Geraldine and shook her hand. "Hello."

Geraldine looked at her closely; she looked relaxed and pretty, very much unlike the frantic voice that she had spoken with on the phone with this morning.

Kelly went over and sat beside her husband.

Geraldine said stiffly, "I don't like to beat around the bush, so I'll just come out and say it. My client would like access to his son."

Theo nodded. "I understand, but technically your client has no parental rights where Mark is concerned. Under Jamaican law a child born into a marriage situation, is in effect the child of the husband unless the couple are estranged or separated, and the biological father can prove his claim on the child via a DNA test, which would have to be obtained by a court ordered. Even then the husband of the relationship will have to declare that he has given away all parental rights to the child and state his reasons. I have no intention of doing so."

Geraldine's eyes widened. "So you have done some research?"

Theo nodded. "In effect, Chris has no case. Getting married was a long shot for him. And even then, he would have to prove that Mark is being ill-treated and is not being cared for properly in order to get access—much less custody."

Geraldine settled back in her chair drumming her fingers. "I came here to inform you that Chris is serious about getting access and I will do everything in my power to see he's successful. Will you volunteer for Mark to do a DNA test?" she asked them both.

Theo shrugged, "Mark is Chris' biological son there is no need for a DNA test."

Geraldine huffed inside. She thought they would have been scared at the thought of her coming but they were looking at her confidently and she felt like a novice.

"Well, this is a warning." She got up forcefully. "I will not stop until Chris gets access to the child."

Theo nodded. "It doesn't have to come to court cases and threats. We can have dialogue with Chris, without lawyers."

Geraldine nodded and wished them both a good evening. Theo showed her out.

"You showed her," Kelly said grinning.

Theo smirked. "Textbook stuff—Now you need to call Chris to call her off, until we decide what to do."

*****

The next morning Kelly dialed Chris' number reluctantly.

She had really thought that this whole scenario would never need to happen. She had wished that Chris could be swept under the rug and treated like a mistake that she shouldn't have made.

The phone rang several times throughout the day unanswered. Then at twelve a breathless jovial voice came on the line.

"Speak to me, baby."

Kelly smiled. Chris would have a handful with this girl. Then she frowned, her son would be in this woman's life, she would need to know more about her.

"Is Chris there?" Kelly asked abruptly, feeling angry all over again that he had the audacity to send a lawyer to try to scare her.

"Nope," the person on the other end said cheerfully.

Kelly asked hesitantly. "Who is this?"

"This is Mrs. Chris Donahue."

"Oh," Kelly said stiltedly. "The woman who he married just so he could get access to my son."

There was a very loud inhalation and then the voice on the line became serious. "Is this Kelly?"

"Yes," Kelly said feeling sorry that she had blurted out what she was thinking. For all she knew Chris loved his wife, and his trying to get custody was just a weird coincidence.

"Chris is not here," Pinky said softly. "I'll tell him you called though."

Kelly felt ashamed. The poor girl sounded wounded, like a bad bully had just socked her a punch.

"I am sorry that I said what I said," Kelly said, repentantly. "I am going to blame it on pregnancy hormones…I'm a bit more emotional and mean these days. Can you give him my number and ask him to call please?"

She gave Pinky the number and when she hung up. Kelly

felt uneasy. She was sure she heard a sob before the phone was put down. She shrugged it off.

Chapter Thirteen

Pinky was sitting in the living room. The lights were turned down really low and the television was muted. She was curled up in a sofa, feeling vulnerable and wounded. She had cried today and her face was puffy and swollen.

She was tired from all the crying though and she felt pathetic. Why hadn't she realized that it all came back to Kelly?

When Chris had said he needed her that was not idle talk; he had really needed her to get this custody show on the road.

She felt a loss so heavy it was actually pressing down on her chest. She imagined herself having a heart attack right in the middle of the chair and Chris coming in to find her dead. The thought of his suffering brought a smile to her lips and she wondered if she had finally gone mad.

She sat up in the settee straighter. This was all her fault. She had married Chris knowing that he had other emotional commitments. For a foolish moment she had thought that he had finally pushed them aside.

She sniffed. In the whole scheme of things, it was admirable that Chris couldn't or wouldn't callously give up his child for others to raise. He wanted to get to know him so badly that he was willing to get married for it. Except in this scenario, she hadn't been consulted about this whole thing. She felt deceived. She had really and truly been sucked into Chris' damaged sphere as her brother had warned her.

Maybe that's why his mother was so standoffish, maybe the poor woman didn't approve of the way Chris was handling things.

Pinky sat up straighter and stared at the television absentmindedly. Her final exams would start in four weeks, and she had to present her latest science project in four days before a group of her peers and the teachers of the chemistry department.

She had been leaning more toward cosmetic chemistry and for her final project she had chosen to make a hair relaxer.

She had to show, from scratch, how she obtained potassium hydroxide from wood ash and then show the exact formula she used to achieve a creamy end product, which by her calculations could penetrate the protein structure of the hair by up to 70% without severely weakening the cortical layer of the hair.

It was simple stuff for a final year chemistry student and she had done everything from scratch. She had used some in her hair today after testing it on several Afro wigs for weeks and found that it really worked.

She had been ecstatic until she answered the phone and was reminded that she may be good at school chemistry, but where relationship chemistry was concerned, she was a failure.

She had even deceived herself into thinking Chris was happy. How delusional could a girl get?

"There you are!" Chris said walking into the room his tie was askew and his hair ruffled. He looked adorable though slightly weary around the eyes. Usually she would greet him effusively but she sat in the sofa looking at him sadly.

"What's wrong? Who died?" Chris asked urgently.

"My rose colored spectacles." Pinky said mournfully. Chris sat beside her and kissed her on the cheek.

"What on earth did I do wrong? You look like you've been crying."

"I was." Pinky said looking at him her eyes tearing up again. "First I was so happy. I finally made hair relaxer with a weak alkaline agent, all by myself."

Chris nodded puzzled. "Congrats, that's for your final project right?"

"Right," Pinky sniffled, "then Kelly called."

Chris inhaled sharply. "She did?"

"Yup," Pinky nodded. "I found out that... this...ours is a marriage of convenience. That she is pregnant and that you are planning to fight them for custody of your son."

Chris sighed and leaned back in the settee. His mind was racing; what could he say? He had not told her the truth about this hasty marriage. He hadn't allowed her to make up her mind about it. He had reasoned that if he married anyone else she would have been devastated. He was right but what he did was really a deception.

"I am guilty." He looked at her sorrowfully. "My lawyer suggested it. I really have little recourse if I want to see my son, but I couldn't see myself marrying anyone else."

"I am not going to shout. Curiously, I have little energy for that sort of thing. My main feeling right now is that I was betrayed." She fidgeted with her fingers. "I am going to move in with Charles for a bit."

"No," Chris growled, "I want you here. Why are you leaving?"

"Because," Pinky said slowly, "I have exams in two-weeks. This whole thing is a distraction I can well do without. I want to get my degree, I am going to be terribly heart broken in the future and I'll need an education to fall back on."

"Pinky, don't talk like that," Chris said urgently, "and don't walk out on our marriage."

"I am not walking out," Pinky said standing up, "I just need a break. I am not even taking my clothes. Well, only a few pieces for the next couple of weeks. I have some serious lab work to do handling some combustible chemicals. I can't afford for this whole business to distract me, okay. I know you don't love me, I had at least hoped you like me just a little bit to want to see me do well in school."

The protest that Chris was about to make died rapidly at that plaintive plea. If he protested now she would be reading it as him not even liking her. He watched her walk out of the room her shoulders slumped, but he had this urge to beg her not to leave him. Every time she left the house it was like an empty space opening wider in his chest.

Chapter Fourteen

Chris was tired of the stilted conversations with Pinky over the phone. It was going on for two weeks. She had her final exam today and then he was going to Flatbush for her. He missed her like crazy. He could barely concentrate and he was hardly eating. Even the cat was walking around the place with his tail drooping—the two of them making a sad pair.

Pinky had forbidden him from visiting her. She had used the, 'if you like me, you would want to see me do well' argument. He heard the sadness in her voice and had relented but he wanted to see her face, to touch her skin, to see her facial expressions and bask in the high voltage energy that was Pinky.

Today he was going to put a stop to this estrangement. He didn't like it. Geraldine had called him a few days ago and told him about her conversation with Theo and Kelly. Apparently they refused to be scared into anything. They knew their legal rights and weren't willing to be browbeaten by big, bad Geraldine. He had laughed when she said 'big bad Geraldine'.

He propped up Kelly's number on his desk; he hadn't had the urge to call her yet. A part of him was reluctant to hear her voice. A part of him didn't want to know what she had to say because he was sure it would be negative for him.

He leaned back in his chair and thought about her objectively. The very thought that he could do that gave him pause. Whatever it is that had him in a grip of Kelly obsession was gone. He hadn't even realized that it was gone.

He poked around the wound that had Kelly's name on it and realized that it was mostly scar tissue. Not even a pinch of pain when the memories of their affair came flooding back. He thought about her smiling over his desk in only his shirt. He remembered the day they spent in bed together when Theo had gone to a conference. Like a blind fool he had pretended that they were married.

The memories dangled across his mind one-by-one and he reviewed them realizing something vitally important. It hadn't been about love. It had been about winning. It had been about revenge and what he considered to be delayed justice because Theo had the audacity to take his girl.

He had been arrogant and egotistical and he had stayed that way for years, brooding and unhappy. All those years wasted but then again probably not, he had to wait for Pinky to grow up because frankly he could not see himself with anybody else.

He counted down the time until he could go and pick her up from Flatbush. One thing was for sure he wasn't going to sleep another night without his wife.

*****

Chris followed Pinky's car until it parked up at the gate on Flatbush Scheme. She got out of her car and dashed inside the house with a sickly look on her face. He hurriedly braked behind her car and dashed in the house after her. She had even left the front door wide opened. He heard her retching in the bathroom. He appeared in the bathroom doorway and she was on her knees over the toilet.

He became alarmed. "What's wrong?"

Pinky flushed the toilet and got up shakily. "Food poisoning I guess. It's the weirdest thing but I haven't been eating much and then I feel like crap in the evenings."

"So if you haven't been eating, how can it be food poisoning? Chris frowned "You look like hell warmed up."

"Thanks." Pinky slowly reached for her toothbrush. "I feel like hell."

Chris whipped out his phone. "We are going to see the family doctor." He moved away from the bathroom and made an appointment with Dr. Mansfield.

"He's expecting us in an hour," Chris said with concerned that Pinky didn't look so good and actually appeared to have lost some weight--a lot of weight. How could she have lost so much weight in such a short space of time?

He felt like a heel. He had done this to her. She looked like somebody who had been beaten up by life and was left defeated.

She slowly walked to the small bedroom on their right and sat down on the bed. "I feel weak."

She closed her eyes briefly then opened them again. "I had my last exam today—yay!" Her voice was thready and the intended enthusiasm sounded faint.

"I know," Chris said, leaning up at the door, "I came to escort you home. Where's your brother?"

"He's hardly here," Pinky said faintly, "he's a management

trainee now. They have him living on the hotel property most of the time."

"I am going to call to have him drop off your car at the house later. You are going to the doctor, then to the house where you belong."

Pinky didn't argue, she really felt weak and out of sorts. Over the last few days she had done her exams under a cloud of sickness, with sheer grit and determination she had completed the last exam today.

Her friends had wanted her to go to celebrate but she had felt her stomach roiling with nausea and she had hurriedly jumped into the car to reach home. She felt sick and faint and quite anti-social.

She hardly remembered getting into Chris' car. She barely registered that he was looking concerned. Between periods of sleepiness, a pounding head and dry retching, she could vaguely recall being wheeled onto a trolley. She couldn't even speak. A welcome darkness was holding onto her, sucking out her strength and making her limbs weak.

*****

"What's the matter with her?" Chris was pacing in the private clinic thirty-minutes after Dr. Mansfield, had taken one look at Pinky, felt her pulse and called an ambulance.

Chris had driven like a mad man behind the ambulance until it had reached the private facility.

"She has hyperemesis gravidarum otherwise called HG." Dr. Mansfield looked at him over his glasses.

Chris stopped pacing long enough to feel a wretched fright descend over him. "Is that something serious? Is she going to die?"

"It can be serious," Dr. Mansfield said, "she was severely

dehydrated when you brought her in, so we have her on IV hydration right now. She is showing signs of recovering. Hyperemesis gravidarum is a rare complication of pregnancy and it is yet to be seen how long this will last, or what triggers it. We'll need to keep her here and monitor her for a while."

"Pregnancy?" Chris felt light-headed. He looked at the doctor and felt a surreal sensation grip his body. He hadn't expected pregnancy; of all the things the doctor could have said pregnancy was the last thing on his mind.

How could it be? Pinky was on the Pill. She'd gone on it a day before they got married.

Dr. Mansfield patted him on the shoulder. "Congratulations young man. You can go in and see your wife shortly."

Chris nodded absently and then sat down on a waiting room chair. It was plush and comfortable; he was the only one in there. He curled his hand in his hair and tugged it a little to release the pressure in his brain. He was going to be a father again. Happiness warred with the fear in his mind, but this time he was going to get it right, if Pinky survived.

The unbidden thought sneaked up on him that maybe Pinky was being punished for his past sins but he stamped it down fiercely. He took a deep breath and headed toward the room where Pinky was. Each step became lighter until when he pushed her door opened. His smile was as wide as could be.

*****

When Pinky opened her eyes, she felt as if she had been in a stampede with large bulls. Hyacinth Donahue was sitting at the side of her bed reading a book.

Her bed? She looked around she was in a gaily painted room.

"Where am I?" she asked looking at Hyacinth quizzically.

It hurt to turn her head, as if it had been in a particular position too long.

"In a private clinic, dear." Hyacinth said to her kindly.

"I was that sick?" Pinky asked huskily, her throat felt dry and gravelly. "Do I have the flu?"

Hyacinth leaned over to her. "I am going to ring for the nurse. They told me to call them as soon as you wake up."

"Where's Chris?" Pinky asked slowly. Her tonsils felt swollen, or was it her throat? She was hooked up to two different IV's.

"Chris went home to freshen up," Hyacinth said gently. "He brought you in yesterday evening. He had them bring in a cot so he could sleep in here with you. He had to go home this morning so I offered to sit in. He'll be back shortly."

A nurse came through the door briskly. "Mrs. Donahue, I am Nurse Foster, I see you are up."

Pinky blinked, except for Maud, she couldn't remember anyone calling her Mrs. Donahue.

"Er...what's wrong with me?" she asked the nursed urgently. "I feel really weird."

"You have a rare pregnancy complication," The nurse said simply. "I am going to take your vital signs."

"I am not pregnant," Pinky giggled weakly.

"Two tests say you are," the nurse said smiling. "You are eight weeks along."

Pinky looked at Hyacinth wide-eyed.

Hyacinth smiled reassuringly.

"But I was on the Pill."

The nurse adjusted a blood pressure cuff on her arm. "These things happen. I see it all the time."

Pinky closed her eyes. Her mind was slowly processing this revelation. She was married to a man who didn't love her and then she had the added bonus of burdening him with a child. Her heart leapt in fear. What on earth was going on?

"Relax," the nurse said soothingly, "it's alright. Your blood pressure is shooting off the charts."

Pinky drew in a deep breath and then another. Then she looked at Hyacinth Donahue's face and then panicked again.

"Mrs. Donahue," the nurse said turning to Hyacinth, "can you leave us for a minute please?"

"Sure," Hyacinth said standing up.

When she left the nurse looked at Pinky solemnly. "Big news huh?"

Pinky nodded. "Very big. I can't wrap my mind around it. A baby? Oh heavens, I can't even take care of myself properly."

The nurse shushed her. "Take in a deep breath and repeat after me, 'the Lord is my shepherd….'"

"The Lord is my shepherd," Pinky said obediently.

"I shall not want."

Pinky repeated Psalm 23 until she was calm again.

"Thank you." Pinky looked at her gratefully.

"No problem honey." The nurse winked. "I sing on the choir with Miss Hyacinth at Three Rivers Church. Maybe you can convince Chris to come back to our church, since he's now married and about to start a new family. The church family would love to see him."

Pinky nodded. "I'll tell him."

Chapter Fifteen

Pinky stayed in the clinic for a full two weeks but couldn't keep anything down. She had such intense nausea and vomiting and was dropping weight so rapidly that her doctor, an obstetric gynaecologist, Sarah Ogilvie, was worried.

A haggard looking Chris was sitting across from her while she rummaged through her notes.

"I think we should terminate," Sarah looked over her glasses, "Petrina is losing weight too rapidly. This pregnancy might kill her if we don't do something in the next forty-eight hours."

Chris heaved a sigh. It was early morning, almost half past six. He had slept over at the clinic last night to keep Pinky company as usual. Not that she had noticed much. She was so ill. The doctor had done her rounds at five o' clock and was looking very concerned.

Chris looked at her wearily. "Forty eight hours you say?"

Sarah nodded. "This is quite serious and I would not have

mentioned termination if that was not a last resort."

Chris nodded slowly, his head feeling heavy as if it was twice its normal size.

He went into the room where Pinky was staying. She was lying very still. He frantically looked over her body to see if there was any sign of movement under the sheet.

She finally shifted and he breathed a sigh of relief. Just yesterday, she had said, that it hurt even to swallow and she had gotten so worryingly thin. Chris sat beside the bed and took up her hand gently.

"Pinky," he whispered, "please don't die. Dr. Ogilvie says that if we don't take the baby you could die. I would much rather you were around."

He felt his eyes water up. This girl had come to mean so much to him that the thought of her not being around filled him with an emptiness and despair that was enough to make him grit his teeth in agony.

Pinky's eyes fluttered open. She smiled at him weakly. "Hey, are those tears husband?"

Chris wiped his eyes. "Yes they are."

"So, it's either the baby or me, huh?" She grimaced in pain while she tried to shift.

"No," Chris shook his head, "there is no choosing at the moment. It's just you."

Pinky swallowed shakily, "I know this pregnancy was a surprise to both of us, but I've been getting used to the whole thing in the past couple of days."

"Me too." Chris said sadly kissing her hand.

"I think we should ask God to guide us." Pinky closed her eyes weakly. "He is the Great Physician isn't he?"

Chris nodded and then realizing that she couldn't see him cleared his throat. "Yes He is."

"And He's your friend isn't He?" Pinky asked her voice

cracking up.

"Well... He was," Chris said uncomfortably. "I mean, we were close until I had that affair, and then I deceived you... my whole life has gone down hill since then."

Pinky drifted off to sleep and Chris placed the hand he was holding gently on the bed.

She stirred after Chris sat there for torturous minutes contemplating his closeness to God. "You know what my favorite text in the whole Bible is."

"What?" Chris whispered.

"Hebrews 10. Especially verse 22." She opened her eyes, "I even know it by heart, it says 'Let us draw near with a true heart in full assurance of faith, having our hearts sprinkled from an evil conscience, and our bodies washed with pure water.' Pray for us Chris, I have the faith that God will work this out according to his will."

Chris closed his eyes and got down on his knees beside Pinky's bedside and prayed a heartfelt prayer to God, the likes of which he had not prayed for years.

*****

The forty-eight hour deadline was extended, because according to Sarah Ogilvie it was a miracle that Pinky was actually doing better.

Chris heaved a sigh of relief; the great physician had heard his request. He had no doubt that it was God's doing—a very loud wake up call to him.

He had, for the first time in years, sat down unselfishly and thought about his life. It was a humbling experience. He had felt so disgusted with how self-absorbed he had become—so arrogant and so misguided.

It was because of his selfishness that he had that affair. It

was even because of that same selfishness that he had wanted
Mark. God had shown him what it was like to be on the brink
of losing a child within his marriage, and he had finally seen
how Kelly and Theo must have been feeling.

The whole experience had been illuminating and he
realized where he could have spared himself a lifetime of
bad choices if he had just put God first. The equation was
so simple but he had paid lip service to it. He had even told
people the same thing but he hadn't been practicing. He had
read Hebrews 10, Pinky's favorite chapter and he could see
hope and chastisement in there for him.

Chris walked out of the clinic with a new vigor in his gait.
He had no doubt that God had forgiven him and had heard
his prayers.

When he got home that evening his house was packed with
family and friends.

Pinky's parents had come over in the morning and had
been taking turns visiting Pinky and then sleeping over at
his house.

Charles and Tanya were there as well; Caleb was in his
kitchen fixing dinner. Chris had never seen his house filled
with so many people before, all of them concerned about
Pinky. The Three Rivers Church brethren had even set up a
prayer vigil the day before.

His mother was in the living room holding court with
several people. He spotted Erica and -- his eyes widened—
Phoebe. He hadn't seen her since her wedding.

"How is she?" his mother asked when he entered the living
room.

"Doing better." Chris looked at them wearily. "The doctor
thinks that she's showing signs of improvement. Thank you
for your prayers."

"Ah," Erica said bouncing her baby on her legs, "don't

mention it."

He left them all to their chatting, the place had taken on a convivial atmosphere after his announcement and he could hear laughter and even music as Charles took to the piano. He headed for the kitchen where Caleb was in there alone whistling.

"Hey man." He glanced up at Chris.

"You are working overtime." Chris grinned at him.

"Heard that my friend and boss needed support, so here I am. Your kitchen is really nice by the way," Caleb said stirring a pot and sprinkling some seasoning in it. "Maud was going to fix sandwiches but I couldn't stand the thought of something so simple, so I volunteered to cook. You have quite the crowd out there."

"It's appreciated man." Chris sat on a stool at the island and proceeded to peg a tangerine. "I had an epiphany today."

"Oh." Caleb looked back at him. "What was it?"

"That God has a unique way of teaching His wayward children a lesson."

Caleb nodded. "He does. My life is a testimony to that."

"I am going to call off this whole custody battle I was planning against Theo and Kelly."

Caleb grinned, "I knew you would figure it out that way. There are just some things you need to move on from."

Chris nodded. "You are so right."

Chapter Sixteen

Pinky spent two months in the hospital. When she came back home, it was with a nurse in tow. She would have to be monitored for the duration of her pregnancy because she was still not gaining weight as rapidly as she should.

"I can't believe I am going to be cooped up like this for a whole four months." She cradled the small mound in front of her. "I hardly even look pregnant. Shouldn't I be huge?"

Charles, who was visiting smirked. "You couldn't wait to come out of the clinic. You said you wanted a familiar environment and your husband bent over backwards to get the doctors to agree. Stop complaining."

"He's been good hasn't he?" Her eyes lit up. "I have never seen him so tender."

"He loves you," Charles said flinging one foot over the armchair facing her bed.

"No he doesn't," Pinky retorted, "he loves children. I'm

the person carrying his next one. So I have to be treated with care."

Charles frowned. "Have you guys talked about the whole situation Pinky? Cause it seems to me that Chris has no thought or time for anything else but you and your comfort."

Pinky smiled reluctantly. "He's been so good, I think I love him a teensy bit more everyday."

"Ah," Charles said, "I am sure he feels the same way."

"And I am sure he doesn't," Pinky sighed. "He would have bent over backward for anyone carrying his child. I am his chance at a second fatherhood."

Charles shook his head. "I don't know anything much about Chris and his thought processes but he doesn't look like a man who is merely going through the motions."

"He loves Kelly," Pinky said softly. "When they were dating he wrote poems for her, and treated her like a queen and when you call her name he has this look in his eyes, and he mourned her for years. That's the kind of look I want for myself."

Charles shrugged, "Howie and the crew want to know if they can come and visit you tomorrow?"

"Sure," Pinky said nodding, "I miss them. I miss the sea. Wish I could go swimming now."

"Don't you dare." Charles got up and kissed her on the cheek. "I am going to get a milkshake, want one?"

"No." Pinky shuddered. "I can't stand the sight or scent of most food, just imagining the scent of milk shake is enough to make me gag."

"Okay soon be back," Charles said. "I will drink it downstairs. Maybe we can watch Star Trek reruns together when I come back."

Pinky grinned. "You know that I must be near death's door when my brother will sit down and watch Star Trek with me."

Charles sloped his shoulders, and looked   at her lovingly. "When Chris told us that you could die I was so scared." He averted his watering eyes from her. "Soon be back."

Pinky settled back into the bed and closed her eyes. She was getting better, but she wasn't happy. The doctor had warned her about being stressed and so she tried to think happy thoughts. But she had this niggling feeling, at the back of her mind, that Chris didn't love her. He liked her, she couldn't deny that, and he wanted his baby alive and well. But love? He wasn't that into her. The thought made her squirm inside and was starting to take up a big space in her thought processes.

Chapter Seventeen

Chris sat in his study whirling his chair around, his thoughts going back and forth with the whirling motions of the chair. It was August 5th. Today was Mark's birthday. He hadn't even bothered to go into the office early. The company had acquired a large tract of prime real estate just yesterday— over a hundred acres. He had bargained hard to get the land and knew it was going to be spectacular, whatever the board decided to do with it. He earned some down time and he was delaying going into the office.

Pinky was treating him super friendly and distant. He had tried to breach her determined friendliness and have them really communicate with each other but she was treating him as she did in the days when she used to work as his housekeeper. It was a defensive attitude, all her walls were up and he wanted to know how to tear them down.

What had he done to warrant this sudden defensiveness?

He couldn't really harass her for answers; she was seven months pregnant and still suffering from HG. She was still under constant supervision by a nurse and was still weak. She walked like an invalid and looked so delicate, like a small wind could blow her over.

He was not into bullying her to talk to him; she was a mere shadow of her former sparkly self. And he had this foreshadowing guilt that he had caused this on her. She was like a nice shiny toy that he had broken. Their reason for marrying was no longer relevant. He didn't want to pursue custody of Mark anymore. He clenched his teeth. The desire to do so was still there, but he wouldn't.

He had been so preoccupied with work and taking care of his sick wife that he hadn't even called back Kelly. He had already told Geraldine to tell them that he had changed his mind.

He hadn't seen a reason to call Kelly. He recited her number in his head. He could call her now; maybe he could get a sliver of information about Mark. He was drumming his finger on the desk and then he took up his cell phone.

The phone rang three times and then she came on the line. Her sweet voice wrapped around him evoking memories he thought he had buried.

"Hi Kelly."

"Chris!" Kelly exclaimed, she had waddled to the phone from the living room, she was supposed to give birth to Luke any day now. They had done an ultra sound and found out the sex of the baby. Theo's head popped up from the magazine he was reading at her exclamation. He was on vacation for four weeks and was at home with her.

"I am just returning your call from a few months ago." Chris cleared his throat.

"I understand," Kelly said sitting down inelegantly on the

side of the bed, "I heard that Pinky was not doing so well. How is she now?"

"She is being monitored," Chris said uncomfortably. Talking to Kelly after all this time made him feel vulnerable and weird.

"It's Mark's fourth birthday, time really flies." He cleared his throat. "I guess it would be inappropriate to tell him happy birthday."

Kelly was silent for a long while and then she heaved a sigh, "that's why I called you so many months ago. Theo and I decided that Mark should get to know your side of the family."

"Are you serious?" Chris exclaimed excitedly. "I can get to know my son?"

"Yes," Kelly said, "you can. Theo thinks it would be morally unfair to deny you the right to get to know him."

"Oh thank you," Chris said relieved. "Thank you, guys." He got up from his chair suddenly energized.

"Theo thought that since the family will be coming out in December that you could be introduced to him, and maybe spend a day or so together. After that you can get some time with him in summer when the children come to Jamaica in the summer. Sorry, that's the best we can do."

"That's a lot!" Chris said humbled. "I never expected this."

Kelly shrugged and realized that he couldn't see her. "I hear how happy you are, I must apologize for being a pain over this. I wanted to cut you out altogether, you know, let you suffer for our mistake."

Chris sighed. "You know Kelly, you were my first love. I had never felt that way before and..."

He heard a thud outside and he went to the door. It was Pinky sitting on the floor with a look of fear in her eyes.

"I didn't mean to eavesdrop," she said painfully. "I was

honestly going to knock and come inside when I heard you shouting for joy."

Chris spoke into the phone. "Kelly, I'll call you back."

"You can call back in the evening," Kelly said softly. "I'll tell Mark that a special friend wants to wish him happy birthday."

"Thanks." Chris said hanging up the phone hurriedly.

Pinky was looking shell-shocked. "So you are going to get access to your son and you are professing your love for Kelly."

Chris opened his mouth in shock and then snapped it shut. "It's not like that."

"Then what is it like?" Pinky asked tears in the corner of her eyes, "I guess you don't want this baby or me either. Kelly crooked her little finger and you are off declaring your love and planning happy families with her."

Her breathing was shallow and Chris was watching her cautiously. If it was one thing he knew about a hysterical female was that telling them to keep calm didn't work and approaching them usually elicited a violent reaction.

"I am not going to play happy family with Kelly," he said calmly. "She's due to give birth any day now, and with a child for her husband."

Pinky looked at him with tear washed eyes. "I'm ugly aren't I? I can hardly move and I am sick." She curved her arms around her belly. "I bet Kelly is blooming with her pregnancy."

Chris advanced to her rapidly. "Pinky you are beautiful, you've always been."

"I am going to take my baby and leave." She said hysterically,

The nurse had heard the commotion and came swiftly down the stairs.

"Mrs. Donahue, you shouldn't be upsetting yourself like this, you'll go into premature labor."

"Tell that to my husband," Pinky panted when the nurse helped her up. "He wants me to die so that he can be free to marry his first love," she sneered.

Chris rolled his eyes when the nurse looked at him swiftly. "Isn't today the day we are supposed to be going for the ultrasound?"

Pinky sobbed. "You don't love me, you only want me for a brood mare."

Chris chuckled. "I can't want you for a brood mare and want to get rid of you at the same time."

Pinky leaned on the nurse, "all I want is to be loved for me," she hiccupped.

Chris held out his hand to touch her but she almost stumbled to get away from him. "Don't touch me Christopher Donahue. Me and my baby are only second best."

Chapter Eighteen

So that was it; the crux of her standoffish attitude?

All through the ultrasound, when they discovered that they were going to have a girl. All through the eighth months of her pregnancy he tiptoed around her because he didn't want anything stressful to tip her off. She was so ill, she was allergic to prenatal vitamins and in her eighth month she became swollen all over.

He wanted her to have a safe delivery, so he said nothing, their conversations though were bordering on the ridiculous. Pinky only spoke to him when she absolutely had to. She had him in a slight panic about whether she was going to run off when she had the baby.

When he had suggested decorating the nursery in pink, Pinky looked at him balefully, "I don't think we'll be here."

He counted to ten in his mind, gave her one of his patient smiles, and tucked the sheet around her legs, "Pinky, you can't just run off with my baby."

"But Kelly did it," Pinky said petulantly, "and you still love her, don't you?"

Chris inhaled and exhaled rapidly. He was on the verge of losing control. He bit his lips and then got up from the bed and started to pace. He refused to shout at her but she had descended into a spoilt brat.

He looked at her hostilely. "If you want me to love you, this is not the way to go about it. You are acting like a...a... excuse me." He slammed out of the room.

Pinky sobbed for the rest of the day. She had pushed him too far; she could see the hatred in his eyes just now. She had wanted some type of reaction from him, and now she had gotten it. She wished she hadn't pushed so hard. Now he didn't even seem as if he liked her.

She looked in the mirror; she looked a mess and even her nose was swollen. At least her hair was longer than she had seen it in years. So there was some advantage to being pregnant—she had about six inches of hair growth. She had clipped off her hair ends and her natural hair was lush and lovely.

As soon as she had the baby she would relax it and dye it purple. She changed her mind almost immediately—maybe red, or burnt orange, or leave it natural and rock, the same kind of natural hairstyle that Kelly had. Maybe she could copy Kelly's hairstyle and see if that would work for her.

She went searching for Chris to tell him sorry and found him in the room next door. He had removed all the furniture in there and was looking over a paint chart. Her heart clenched fiercely when she saw him. He was so handsome and manly with his rolled up denim shirtsleeves and his worn jeans.

"I think Brea would love yellow." She said from the doorway.

Chris' head snapped up and he looked at her wearily. "I

was thinking light pink."

"That's so girly girl."

"Oh so we are not thinking of having a girly girl and we are naming her Brea?"

Pinky nodded. "Brea Christina Donahue."

Then she said hesitantly. "Sorry, Chris, for my outburst earlier."

"And last month and the month before that?" Chris said looking down at the charts.

Pinky sighed. "It gets to me to know that I am...never mind."

Chris looked up at her. "You're what?"

"I am a shrew..." Pinky finished weakly, she wanted to say not loved but how pathetic can one girl get? She kept harping on about it the further he retreated from her.

Chris smiled, his hazel eyes lighting up, "I have argued that all of this is due to hormones and I have reasoned that maybe this is God's way of making me more patient. So you have actually done me a favor."

Pinky smirked, "okay."

He looked at her, a serious look in his eye. "I want to talk to you."

"About what?" Pinky fiddled with the end of her gown.

"About Mark."

Pinky sighed. "What about him?"

"Theo and Kelly have agreed that he can spend summers with us. I guess his time would be divided among his two sets of grandparents and here, and with Erica and Caleb."

"Congrats." Pinky said painfully.

"This concerns you too Pinky."

"I don't see why," Pinky said faintly, "it's not as if I will be here for much longer. Nor did I have a say in this cozy arrangement."

Chris exhaled and then looked back at the paint samples.

"Your reason for marrying me is no longer valid. I guess I'll just have to go back to my parents place, find a job and move on with my life."

Chris looked up at her threateningly. "You are not leaving this place with my child. I am not losing another child. Do you understand me?" He clenched his teeth. "I am sick and tired of your threats. I thought you came in here to apologize."

Pinky swung away frightened. She had never seen Chris look so angry, almost murderous. He looked like a man that had reached the end of his tether. Then a pain hit her from the bottom of her belly, a pain so sharp she gasped out loud with it.

"Pinky, are you alright?" Chris asked concern lacing his voice.

"I think I am having the baby," Pinky said fearfully.

Chapter Nineteen

When Brea Christina Donahue came into the world, Chris was right there with Pinky. There were three doctors attending. Dr. Ogilvie was fearful that Pinky would have complications but Brea was fine. She weighed 3 kg. She was on the small side but everybody breathed a sigh of relief when she was born, especially Chris, who had panicked when Pinky had gone into labor.

He was staring at her now, his little pink bundle, and he bent close to her face to check that she was breathing. His heart swelled with love when he looked at her. It was pure love. He had only felt this way once before, when Mark was born, but that situation had been rife with uncertainty and guilt.

This feeling was perfect. He looked at Pinky who was sleeping, her face was blotchy and swollen and it occurred to him that he had never seen her more beautiful. She was crazy if she thought she was going to leave him. His life was just beginning to make sense.

He moved away from the bedside and paced the room a bit. He suddenly wished he hadn't been so dark and moody when he met Pinky. He wished she hadn't known about Kelly because in her head she couldn't measure up and he wasn't sure that she needed to. Pinky was her own unique self. Though she had been exasperating these past few months and testing at times, he wouldn't have had it any other way.

She opened her eyes suddenly and looked down at the baby.

"I can't believe she is really here," Pinky grinned, "and looking like a Donahue."

Chris came over to the bedside. "We have strong genes, don't we?"

Pinky gazed at him, tears suddenly springing to her eyes. "I am sorry."

"For what?" Chris asked.

"For being such a pain," Pinky said, "I need to be more careful of my feelings."

"No." Chris squeezed her hands and she pulled it away.

"Yes, I do or else I will be severely unhappy."

Chris sighed. "Pinky what exactly do you want from me?"

Pinky closed her eyes. "I am feeling weary."

Chris accepted her excuse and sighed loudly. He gazed down at his daughter again and touched her soft downy skin.

*****

Pinky was slowly learning the ropes of motherhood. Her mother had come to stay for a week and Hyacinth Donahue was constantly at the house, sometimes staying overnight. She had made a 180 degree change in attitude toward Pinky and it amazed her how a child could change the attitude of a family member.

The truth be told, Hyacinth had started to thaw toward her from her pregnancy, but now she was unreservedly a part of the family in Hyacinth's eyes.

She had a hard time to get Brea to breast-feed, and the baby was not the most peaceful child on the planet. But when she first opened her eyes Pinky stared into them and she knew why women who were reluctant to give birth suddenly turned into mushy caricatures of themselves.

Pinky found herself brooding and lonely, even when friends came by and there was an outpouring of support from both sides of the family.

Her friends from school and her regular beach crew were constantly calling and she had gotten the all clear from the doctor to go to the beach again, to have sex again and to take up her regular activities. She hadn't gained much weight during her pregnancy and in two months she was at pre-pregnancy size.

She was so lonely though she could taste it. She was yearning for something that she had not had in the first place and that was giving her an intense mental anguish. Chris had become withdrawn from her and she really couldn't blame him. Everything he said she snapped at him. It was as if she couldn't help herself.

It was nearing December and just yesterday, Chris had informed her that Mark would be at some special dinner the Donahues were throwing so that he could meet that side of the family.

Kelly and Theo were going to have him for the Christmas at their house so the day after the Donahues would have him. It was a day with his son, and the news had him so excited that he had been floating on cloud nine ever since.

Pinky felt mean about resenting Mark. She had no rhyme

or reason to do so, but she did.

So there, she admitted it to herself.

That's the reason why she was feeling like a rotten apple for the last few weeks. Mark was the embodiment of all that was wrong with her life. His mother was the beloved Kelly.

She was the standby Pinky who had the stupid nerve to get pregnant with his second best child. Now she would never know if Chris really loved her for her. She would never be the woman who was paramount in his life because even if there was just Kelly to consider, there was now Brea.

The tiny bundle of joy that had Chris wrapped around her little finger.

She was going to be forever the odd woman out in his affections. She briefly considered running away with the baby then once more felt burdened down about her thoughts.

She closed the nursery door and leaned up on it a gigantic sigh escaping her.

Chris was in the opposite doorway that led to the master suite and he folded his arms and looked at her enquiringly.

"I am afraid to ask, but why the sigh?"

"I am sick and tired of being sick and tired." Pinky slouched even further into the door.

"Can we talk?" Chris asked her seriously, "without the hysterics and the snapping?"

"Are you implying," Pinky snarled, "that I am hysterical and snapping?"

Chris nodded contemplatively. "Yes."

"Well, I'm not," Pinky said knowing she was acting exactly how he described, "I am just lonely and unloved. There, I said it!" She moved away from the door. "I know I shouldn't be going on an on about this, but I am human, I can't help it."

Chris sighed. "I don't know what to say to you when you get into this mood."

"Argh." Pinky bared her teeth and then stomped away. "I am not coming to your little Donahue get together next week either. I know all your sisters will be there and your precious son but I think I want to spend Christmas with my family this year. Brea is my parents' grandchild too."

Chris felt the rising anger and tried unsuccessfully to temper it down. "Pinky; stop trying to use Brea as a pawn. I will not be controlled through my daughter no matter how unloved or lonely you feel."

"She is my child," Pinky flung back at him, "I suffered eight months and two weeks through that pregnancy, you didn't do a thing. Mine, all mine."

Chris contemplated following her but then he heard her sobbing down the hallway. If he went to her now she would accuse him of several more crimes, real and imagined.

What had gotten into Pinky? He had even asked her doctor about it. Her doctor said she was going through an intense hormonal upheaval. But surely this constant snarling and crying was not normal behavior?

He had never seen one woman so emotional. She went from normal to depressed in less than a minute and all he had to do was open his mouth to trigger it.

He was so concerned about it that he had started to pray about the matter. He had re-started his devotional life, since that day when he had asked the Lord to save both Pinky and Brea's lives. He realized that God had been too merciful to him for him to forget His mercies and go his own way.

He was drawing closer and closer to God. He went into the room and knelt at his bedside. These days he wasn't taking anything for granted, he felt as if his marriage was on the verge of unraveling all together.

This was something that he had no intention of allowing to happen, so he was going to place his marriage in God's hands and ask him for mercy once more.

Chapter Twenty

Pinky reluctantly went to the Post-Christmas party that the Donahues had planned. Hyacinth had not stopped talking about it for days and a little part of her felt as if she was acting extremely petty to take away the baby when the family had all gathered together even though they were celebrating Mark as if he was the only child in the universe.

Chris had gone to Caleb's and Erica's house two days before to officially be introduced to Mark. Apparently Theo and Kelly had also been there. He hadn't spent long but he had a big old Cheshire grin on his face when he got back.

She had wanted to question him, but the old resentment had almost choked the questions in her. She didn't know if she could have sat by and calmly asked him what happened when he met his other child.

Especially, since his Great Love had been there too. Chris had wanted Pinky to come, but she had told him point blank that she wasn't going to play happy families with him and the child of his affair.

That had hit below the belt and Chris had looked as if he wanted to strangle her, a look she was seeing more often than not. He resisted responding and had valiantly carried on eating. She hadn't seen him for the rest of the day and the curiosity was eating her alive.

It was almost with a sense of relief that when she arrived at the Donahue house, Marie had taken the baby from her and Camille had drawn her to the patio where everybody had gathered.

It was a very happy and relaxed atmosphere and Pinky couldn't help but realize that she was the odd man out. It literally pained her cheekbones to smile. When somebody dropped off Mark and he came onto the patio—with a look of lively curiosity on his face—she didn't even try to crack a smile.

Was she going to be one of those wicked stepmother's? She asked herself honestly. She stood back as the family swooped down on him, giving him welcoming hugs and introducing themselves to him with teary-eyed fervor.

Even Chris was in his element. He was relaxed and smiling and happy. But Pinky felt resentful and peevish.

When Mark had ran inside with his cousins, he didn't take long to get into playing with them. They had commandeered him and he was inside wooing and hollering at the top of his voice.

Pinky realized that she was sitting a bit apart from everybody else. Apparently, they had read her keep off sign and nobody was bothering to trouble her. Harlan had made sure that her apple juice was kept topped up and the rest of the family was tiptoeing around her.

"I would like to propose a toast," Hyacinth was knocking her glass. "This one is for God. He has been good to our family. I'm especially grateful to him that I have all my grandchildren here under the same roof."

"Here, here." Everybody was clinking their glasses and acting all teary eyed.

"I would like to propose a toast." Camille stood up. "To my only baby brother, who finally got it right. Better late than never."

There was laughter and a spattering of talking.

"Thank you Camille," Chris responded. "And I would like to say thank you to my beautiful wife who has given birth to my lovely daughter and for..."

"Just shut up," Pinky said standing up, "you don't have anything to thank me for. I am nothing to you. You love Kelly Palmer, always have—always will. Couple months ago I heard you on the phone telling her just that. I am going to take my child away from here so that you can get on with your life."

She looked at the shocked faces of the family members around and then at Chris who was surveying her grimly.

"You were eavesdropping on a conversation that you did not even hear correctly."

"I heard," Pinky said bristling, "'Oh Kelly, you were my first love.' Tell us, didn't you say that?"

Chris put down his glass on the side table beside him abruptly.

"Pinky, I can't remember what I said. We were discussing me getting access to Mark."

"Mark the prodigal son!" Pinky said a sob in her voice. "You love everybody in this place except me. If it's not Mark, it's Brea, or your parents, or your ex-married-lover. I am so low on the totem pole it doesn't even register."

Chris cleared his throat. "I don't think this is the time or the place."

"Why? Because I ruined your little Prodigal Party?" Pinky looked around wildly, "where's my baby? I want my baby. I am getting out of here."

Chris opened his mouth and then closed it back.

His mother was looking at Pinky in alarm. She reached her first because she had crumpled in the chair crying hysterically.

Camille came and stood beside Chris, a look of concern in her eyes. "How long has this been going on?"

"This was a mistake," Chris said sadly, "I shouldn't have married her. I have destroyed what's good in her. She's like a spoilt child."

"You can't think that way." Marie was holding Brea and came to stand beside Chris. "She's just coming from a difficult pregnancy. She is probably feeling stressed and she is channeling all her anger onto you."

Chris sighed. "How long is this going to last?"

Marie shrugged. "At the clinic where I work the symptoms can last for up to a year. She needs someone to talk to."

Camille looked over at Brea and smiled softly. "I think it's more than stress. That girl feels unloved by you, Chris. Make it right."

"How else can I show that I love her?" Chris said in exasperation. "You guys are acting like I ill-treat her or something. I'm attentive and kind but I get my hand bitten off like she's a rabid dog. If I keep my distance she shouts at me and carries on."

"So maybe you should tell her," Marie said.

They watched as Hyacinth coaxed a sobbing Pinky into the house.

"I doubt that will make a difference," Chris huffed. "I am just unlucky in love that's all."

Chapter Twenty-One

Two weeks after the celebratory dinner where she acted like a shrew and embarrassed Chris and herself, Pinky was filing her nails absently. She was at the back of the house, a gentle breeze was blowing and the day felt quite pleasant.

Maud was humming some tune or the other and Brea was gurgling pumping her little legs in the air and sucking up the attention.

Pinky had really shocked herself into contrition. She had come home subdued and quiet. Chris hadn't spoken to her since then. Deep down, she felt that it was over. No man wanted to be embarrassed in front of his family in such a manner.

Chris hadn't really looked her in the eyes since that evening. He had even moved out of the master suite and into the room down the hall where she had stayed when she had been working for him.

The temperature in the house was below zero. He hadn't

even made an attempt to speak to her. She was really hoping to apologize but feared that she would never get the chance. At least before the party he had made an effort to communicate with her. Now, there was only silence.

She had well and truly run him off.

The feeling of hopelessness at the pit of her stomach was turning into a bigger and even bigger knot everyday. She needed to do something with her time and not be so caught up in her failing relationship with her husband. She was thinking of going back into the lab. Maybe she could do some more of her cosmetic chemistry work. At least the world could benefit from her misery.

She almost jumped, so deep was she in her thoughts, when the phone rang beside her head.

"Hello," she answered gingerly.

"Hey girl." It was Phoebe Hoppings. "I was planning a 'girls only' party. Tanya mentioned that you could be free today at around twelve. Tanya is playing hooky from work for the rest of the day."

Pinky cleared her throat, "I think I'll pass."

"Why?" Phoebe asked curiously.

"Because..." Pinky searched for a good reason, she couldn't claim that she had no one to baby sit. She looked over at Maud who was so engrossed in entertaining Brea that she hadn't even looked up when the phone rang.

"Because..." Phoebe said persuasively.

"I am not good company right now." Pinky said.

"I know," Phoebe laughed, "Tanya said you needed a pick me up."

"Do you and Tanya discuss me?" Pinky asked horrified.

"Of course," Phoebe replied breezily, "she is my best friend. Your brother is her boyfriend. Your name comes up fairly frequently and I must say we are a little concerned."

her voice turned serious. "If you can't come today we are bringing the party to your house."

"Alright, I'll come," Pinky hissed her teeth.

"Twelve o' clock," Phoebe said hurriedly, "I'll tell the security to expect you."

Pinky hung up the phone, the last thing she wanted now was a hen meeting, where they'd peck through her life and make her feel even worse than she was already feeling.

*****

She drove up the road to Phoebe's. They were practically neighbors except that Ezekiel Hoppings owned such a big part of Bluff's Head that she had to drive seven minutes to the main gate. The security waved her through and she parked beside Tanya's car.

"Welcome." Phoebe was at the front door. She gave her a hug and led her to a vast pool area. Tanya was already sitting around a table eating ravenously. Erica Wright was also there, sipping juice. She was the last person Pinky wanted to see, she was the sister of her husband's only love.

She almost spun around but a smiling Phoebe kept a firm hand in the middle of her back and practically shoved her down around the table.

All three women were looking at her with anticipation. Pinky stared at them mutinously.

"Traitor," she spat at Tanya.

Tanya wiped her mouth and belched. "Now what do you expect me to do, your brother is so concerned about you he is putting off singing gigs and sitting around depressed."

"Well," Phoebe said looking at her earnestly, "I became concerned because Erica and Tanya are concerned and I always liked you."

Erica continued sipping her juice slowly and then lowered her glass. "I am just here to tell you that you are a jackass."

"I beg your pardon?" Pinky asked faintly.

"You are a jackass." Erica said sweetly. "You have one of the most handsome men in Three Rivers going crazy over you. Phoebe here stalked him; my own sister had an affair with him at the first opportunity. But he married you. You had his baby. And everyday you get up looking miserable and uncared for. I have insider information," she said at Pinky's speaking look.

"Caleb and Chris are close and Caleb is worried about him. Chris is at his wits end about how to reach you. And here you are acting like a drama queen and driving him crazy. I am on Chris' side. Team Chris all the way."

"He is in love with your sister." Pinky said a spark of hope igniting in her at Erica's frank speech.

"Chris was never in love with Kelly." Erica said rolling his eyes. "He was in lust with her. Like a dog in heat he sniffed her and she refused him for her true mate. He has never gotten it into his thick skull that all of that petrified longing and Shakespearean drama was misguided. He has to come to that conclusion for himself. But when I heard that you are running around claiming that you are unloved, I just had to call you a jackass. I was at your house, the night after Chris found out that you were going to pull through from your sickness. He was so happy he could burst. He gave up that ridiculous custody suit revenge strategy thing with Kelly that night. He had all but given up on seeing Mark."

Erica shook her head. "Girl you are mental."

"I was there that night too," Phoebe said. "He was like a changed man, when he said your name, I thought to myself that Chris has finally found peace."

"I was there that night too," Tanya added earnestly, "Caleb

did a mean chicken curry. I can still taste the delicate combination of pimento and scotch bonnet pepper."

Erica and Phoebe giggled.

"You are off script," Erica said still giggling, "and yes my husband is the best chef this side of Jamaica."

Pinky looked from one of them to the other, she was slowly relaxing. They were a nice set of girls to hang out with, but she had to bring it back to the topic at hand. "Chris only wants Brea, not me."

Phoebe snorted. "When Chris heard that the pregnancy could take your life, he only saw one choice. He told us afterward, that no pregnancy would separate him from his Pinky."

"Really?" Tanya asked misty eyed.

"Really?" Pinky echoed.

"Yes something like that." Phoebe nodded and then confessed, "with a little embellishment." She looked skyward. "Please forgive me."

Erica giggled again. "I smell chocolate."

"Yes," Phoebe said, "I asked my chef, to make some desserts with chocolate especially for you Erica."

Erica nodded. "Good girl. I have trained you well."

Pinky looked over at the buffet. "I guess I could eat something."

"Okay," Phoebe said in relief, "help yourself."

The three ladies watched silently, as she helped herself at the buffet.

Erica whispered to Tanya. "Is Charles really that depressed over Pinky's situation?"

Tanya smiled. "A bit, but I did embellish a little just like Phoebe did."

Phoebe rolled her eyes. "I can't believe I am intervening in Chris Donahue's love life. Why does a perfectly sane human being turn into an idiot over a woman?"

"Didn't Ezekiel buy you an island last week?" Erica asked sarcastically.

"That's because I'm pregnant." Phoebe said grinning. "Oops sorry...that announcement should have come after we sorted out Chris and Pinky."

"Ah," Erica said smiling, "it doesn't matter when it comes. I am so happy for you."

They were hugging and fussing over Phoebe when Pinky came back to the table.

"What's going on?"

"Phoebe is gonna be a Mommy." Erica said excitedly.

"And I'll be right here in Three Rivers throughout the pregnancy," Phoebe said smugly. "I will call upon you guys a lot for advice. I am afraid to ask my Mom for any advice. She will smother the living daylights out of me."

Pinky smiled at Phoebe, "I wish for you a problem free time of it. Lord knows my pregnancy was hell."

"Thanks Hun," Phoebe smiled at her.

*****

Chris came home in the middle of the day. Today was the day when he would hog tie Pinky to a chair and make her listen to him. He was tired of the two of them living like strangers. He was tired of the dogged fear that their marriage wouldn't make it. He was tired of the cold war and today it was going to end, one way or the other.

He stormed into the house.

"Pinky! Pinky!" He bellowed. He ran upstairs. She was not there and the nursery was empty.

So she had really gone with the baby. Panic seized him, and he ran downstairs almost tripping on the last step.

He walked through the kitchen and found Maud at the back, rocking the baby.

"Where's Pinky?" he asked panic lacing his voice.

"Off with her friends." Maud said.

"Which friends?" Chris asked aggressively.

"Er..."Maud scratched her head. The baby began to cry and she hushed her, all the while looking at Chris, who was frantically pacing.

"Hoppings." Maud said finally.

"I didn't know Pinky and Phoebe were friends," Chris asked, "are you sure you heard the name Hoppings."

"Yes," Maud said, "definitely Hoppings."

Chris practically ran towards his car and spun out of his driveway. She made him so mad and tied up inside. He drove up at Ezekiel's gate in record time.

"My wife is in there." He said to the security guard without any preamble, the security was used to seeing him anyway.

"I know," the security said, "let me just alert Mrs. Hoppings that you are here."

He called the house and in what felt like forever, Chris was finally let through the gate.

Phoebe obviously hadn't told Pinky that he was coming because she had opened the door took one look at him and grinned widely.

"Follow me," she said over her shoulder.

He walked rapidly behind Phoebe and onto the patio area. Pinky was chatting around the table with Erica and Tanya. She looked almost normal again and animated like the Pinky he remembered.

He walked up to the table; her back was turned to him. Phoebe had drawn a chair and had sat down hurriedly. She, Tanya and Erica were looking at him with bright curiosity in their eyes.

"Pinky Donahue." He had a thunderous expression on his face.

Pinky spun around, she had noticed that the girls were acting strangely; she gasped. "Is something wrong with Brea?"

"No," Chris said, "listen to me. I don't love Kelly. I got over that a long time ago. I think I got over Kelly when I saw her again in Cayman at Phoebe's wedding."

Pinky's eyes widened.

"I had a thing for one Pinky Black at that time, but I was too stubborn to admit it and too set in my ways to acknowledge it. I..." he ran his fingers through his overlong curls. His hazel eyes were bright with passion.

"I love you and only you. I don't love you because you gave birth to Brea. I don't love you because of whatever insane reason you have concocted in your head. I love you because you are Pinky. The only woman who has ever dredged up so many emotions in this one man."

He took a deep breath. "Whenever, you are not around I feel like the whole world has lost its color. And whenever you are around I feel alive.

"Yes I may have started to say something to Kelly over the phone but I was not going to tell her that I love her now, because I don't. I loved her first, yes and I may have had some problems with detaching myself from that whole experience but I don't love her now. I may not have any corny poems to write to you but the truth is, when I wrote those poems for Kelly, I was young and giddy headed and idealistic. My life is now so much richer because you are in it, even though you drive me crazy sometimes, I enjoy every single moment with you, even your cranky ones.

Tears were running unchecked down Pinky's cheeks.

"Oh Chris that's all I have ever wanted to hear." Pinky got

up and hugged him tightly. "And I am so sorry for the other evening at your parent's house."

Chris kissed her soundly. "You are forgiven."

He arched one eyebrow and looked over her head at the other women who were sitting around the table grinning.

"Was this an intervention?"

"Yup," Erica said nodding. "We took it upon ourselves to intervene in Chris Donahue's love life."

"Well, er, thank you for this time," he grinned, "but next time keep out of my love life. And there'll be a next time, I am sure, with my very highly-strung wife."

They all three nodded enthusiastically.

Pinky hugged him even tighter and he grinned.

Epilogue

Three Rivers Summer Church Bulletin (Week One)

Our very own beloved elder Chris Donahue was re-baptized. His baptism comes after frequent visitations to the church with his beautiful wife Petrina and lovely daughter Brea.

According to elder Chris, he had privately sinned but with public results so he needs to make an outward recommitment to God to let others see the seriousness of his intentions.

He introduced the church to Mark his son with Sister Kelly Palmer, our former pastor's wife.

The picture below shows Mark sleeping on Sister Petrina's lap. Mark will be dividing his time this summer amongst his various relatives. He will also be attending our award-winning Vacation Bible School, which begins in three weeks time.

On a side note: Sister Kelly Palmer gave birth, a few months ago, to a bouncing baby boy that they named Luke. All the best to the family as they go through the gospels.

Congratulations
Very hearty congratulations to Sister Tanya who has finally tied the knot with Great Pond musician, Brother Charles Black. May their union be blessed.

And also a very big congratulation to Brother Charles for his promotion as Entertainment Manager at the Flamingo Hotel.

Prayer Section
Please pray for Sister Phoebe Hoppings who recently found out that she is carrying twins, and her mother who is now attending church. Keep the family in your prayers.

Extra Classes
For six weeks this summer, our very own internationally acclaimed pastry chef Caleb Wright will be giving pastry lessons in the church canteen. Only twenty fortunate persons will be accepted in the class. Certification will be given. Hurry now and sign up.

Reminders
Sister Lola is reminding all choir members that practice will be held at 4 p.m. every Sunday.

Prayer for the week
God, give me grace to accept with serenity
the things that cannot be changed,
Courage to change the things which should be changed
and the Wisdom to distinguish the one from the other.

Living one day at a time,
Enjoying one moment at a time,
Accepting hardship as a pathway to peace,
Trusting that You will make all things right,
If I surrender to Your will,
So that I may be reasonably happy in this life,
And supremely happy with You forever in the next. Amen

THE END

Here's a peek at Brenda's Next Book:
Saving Face

Annette couldn't believe that was it. She gazed at Ryan's scrawny back as he pulled on his clothes and her mind tried to come to terms with the fact that she was no longer a virgin. She had given up her precious virginity for this? The books she had been reading told her that the world would move, her body would shatter in pleasurable pieces, and she would feel complete. She wasn't feeling complete; she was feeling a boatload of guilt and the only thing shattered was her dignity.

Ryan turned around and stared at her, he was feeling uncertain as well. They were both just sixteen. They should've been at choir practice but they had been in his room practicing things of a different kind, and now they were staring at each other a bit shell shocked.

He cleared his throat. "We should get going, Mommy will be home soon."

Annette widened her eyes in consternation, she had only to find her panties which was somewhere on his wooden floor and pull down her skirt.

He had just hiked it up earlier and fumbled and pushed his way into her clumsily. She winced as she got up from the bed—her purity bracelet got caught on the sheets and she tugged it free.

Ryan was wearing one too and the irony of the situation hadn't escaped him. They both could no longer consider themselves members of the church's purity club. They were no longer set apart by their refusal to conform to societal pressures about sex. They were now just regular fornicators, just like those of his peers that previously he would snare at and pity because of their lack of morality.

"Come on," Ryan said harshly. He was hearing the stern

voice of Sister Edna in his ear and his guilt was rapidly multiplying because he saw tears in Annette's eyes.

How could one act—which lasted nearly a minute—be so significant? It wasn't even that good. For one moment in time he had felt a rush of release so sweet and then after that a slap of guilt so sharp he had rolled off Annette's prone body and turned his back to her. It wasn't even worth it, Sister Edna's voice said in his head—in his mind's eye he could see his father nodding in agreement.

Annette wasn't faring any better, she was castigating herself for stopping over at Ryan's. They had been steadily dating for a year and they hadn't gone much past chaste kisses on the cheek and innocent hand-holding, until Ryan had gotten it into his head that he wanted to practice French style kissing—and in this, they had indulged themselves for several weeks.

French kissing had led to breast touching. She should've said something, since she wasn't comfortable with the whole direction into newer and sexier waters. But she had found it pleasant and besides that it wasn't even what they called heavy petting.

Today when she came by to get her choir book from Ryan it was the first time she was even going into his room. It was the first time they had even attempted heavy petting and it was the first time she was having sex. The thought made her shudder…sex wasn't all that it was hyped up to be. Sister Edna, their youth leader, kept telling them to wait and do it God's way, "don't listen to the echoing shouts of the world on the topic." But Annette had guiltily thought that Sister Edna was bitter in her outlook on sex because she wasn't getting any. How wrong she was. It wasn't worth it if you felt like this afterward. No way was it worth it!

"Where's the bathroom?" she asked Ryan. She couldn't look him directly in the face.

"Through there." He pointed to a door in the passageway.

She grabbed her panties and walked gingerly toward it.

She hurriedly wiped up the wetness between her legs and then she washed her face. There was a chipped mirror above the face basin. She tried to avoid staring at herself but she could see that her neatly combed hair was sticking up all over her head.

She wished she hadn't done it. She fixed her hair and then washed her face again. She really wished she hadn't done it.

If only she could time travel. She would just stay at the gate and call Ryan. When he came out she would have just asked him for the book. She wouldn't have come inside his house. She wouldn't have walked into his room and sat on his bed or watched him while he got ready or smiled pleasantly at him while he sat beside her or opened her mouth for that dratted French kiss or laid back on the bed while he leaned over her. She wouldn't have done any of that.

OTHER BOOKS BY BRENDA BARRETT

The Three Rivers Series

Private Sins (Three Rivers Series-Book 1)- Kelly was in deep trouble, her husband was a pastor and she his loyal first lady. Well she was…until she had an affair with Chris; the first elder of their church. And now she was pregnant with his child. Could she keep the secret from her husband and pretend that all was well? Or should she confess her private sin and let the chips fall where they may?

Loving Mr. Wright (Three Rivers Series- Book 2)- A man with a past. A woman who was tired of being single. Erica was tired of searching for the right man, she had all but resigned herself to a single life but then the mysterious Caleb Wright showed up and Erica saw one last opportunity to ditch her single life. He was perfect for her. But what was he hiding? Could his past be that bad that they couldn't get past it?

Unholy Matrimony (Three Rivers Series- Book 3)- The problem: Phoebe was poor and unhappy with her lot. The solution: Marry a rich man and she would be happy. It should be simple, except that her rich suitor, Ezekiel Hoppings, was ugly and her poor suitor, Charles Black, was handsome. But the more she came to know both of them, the more Phoebe realized that some solutions were not as simple as they first appear.

If It Ain't Broke (Three Rivers Series- Book 4)- All Chris Donahue wanted was a place in his child's life. All Pinky Black wanted was his love. Chris Donahue was still obsessed with the married woman he had an affair with and the child they had created together. Though he wanted to, he found that he couldn't move on with his life without his son. Pinky Black knew that Chris' emotions were engaged elsewhere but she wanted him to forget his obsession with Kelly and love her. That shouldn't be so hard? Should it?

Contemporary

Homely Girl- A love to last a lifetime? April and Taj were opposites in so many ways. He was the cute, athletic, boy genius on campus that everybody wanted to be friends with. She was the overweight, shy and withdrawn girl who the bullies teased mercilessly.

But they were friends and the older they got the deeper their friendship became. As friendship turns into something more, does April and Taj have a love that can last a lifetime? Or will time and separate paths rip them apart?

The Preacher And The Prostitute - Prostitution and the clergy don't mix. Tell that to ex-prostitute Maribel who finds herself in love with the Pastor at her church. Can an ex-prostitute and a pastor have a future together?

New Beginnings - When self-styled 'ghetto queen,' Geneva, was contacted by lawyers who claimed that Stanley Walters, the deceased uptown financier, was her father she was told that his will stipulated that she had to live with her sister uptown to forge sisterly bonds. Leaving Froggie, her 'ghetto don,' behind she found herself battling with Pamela her stepmother and battling her emotions for Justin a suave up-towner.

Full Circle- After Diana graduated from school, she had a couple of things to do, returning to Jamaica to find her siblings was top priority. Additionally, she needed to take a well-earned vacation. What she didn't foresee was that she would meet Robert Cassidy and that both their pasts would be so intertwined that disturbing questions would pop up about their parentage, just when they were getting close.

Historical Fiction/Romance

The Empty Hammock- Workaholic, Ana Mendez, was certain that her mother was getting senile, when she said she found a treasure chest in the back yard. After unsuccessfully trying to open the old treasure chest, Ana fell asleep in a hammock, and woke up in the year 1494 in Jamaica! It was the time of the Tainos, a time when life seemed simpler, but Ana knew that all of that was about to change.

The Pull Of Freedom- Even in bondage the people freshly arrived from Africa considered themselves free. Led by Nanny and Cudjoe the slaves escaped the Simmonds' plantation and went in different directions to forge their destiny in the new country called Jamaica.

Jamaican Comedy (Material contains Jamaican dialect)

Di Taxi Ride And Other Stories- Di Taxi Ride and Other Stories is a collection of twelve witty and fast paced short stories. Each story tells of a unique slice of Jamaican life.

CPSIA information can be obtained at www.ICGtesting.com
Printed in the USA
BVOW03s1016150514

353633BV00015B/515/P

9 789769 556607